HIGH HURDLES

Olympic Dreams

Books by Lauraine Snelling

Hawaiian Sunrise

RED RIVER OF THE NORTH

An Untamed Land	*The Reapers' Song*
A New Day Rising	*Tender Mercies*
A Land to Call Home	*Blessing in Disguise*

HIGH HURDLES

Olympic Dreams	*Close Quarters*
DJ's Challenge	*Moving Up*
Setting the Pace	*Letting Go*
Out of the Blue	*Raising the Bar*
Storm Clouds	

GOLDEN FILLY SERIES

The Race	*Shadow Over San Mateo*
Eagle's Wings	*Out of the Mist*
Go for the Glory	*Second Wind*
Kentucky Dreamer	*Close Call*
Call for Courage	*The Winner's Circle*

HIGH HURDLES

Olympic Dreams

LAURAINE SNELLING

BETHANY HOUSE PUBLISHERS
MINNEAPOLIS, MINNESOTA 55438

Olympic Dreams
Copyright © 1995
Lauraine Snelling

Cover illustration by Paul Casale

Published by Bethany House Publishers
A Ministry of Bethany Fellowship International
11400 Hampshire Avenue South
Minneapolis, Minnesota 55438
www.bethanyhouse.com

Printed in the United States of America by
Bethany Press International, Minneapolis, Minnesota 55438

Library of Congress Cataloging-in-Publication Data

Snelling, Lauraine.
    Olympic dreams / Lauraine Snelling.
        p.   cm. — (High hurdles ; bk. 1)
    Summary: Thirteen-year-old DJ needs God's help in achieving her dream of getting a horse and competing as a show jumper in the Olympics.

    [1. Horses—Fiction. 2. Olympics—Fiction. 3. Christian life—Fiction.] I. Title. II. Series: Snelling, Lauraine. High hurdles ; bk. 1.
PZ7.S67701   1995
[Fic]—dc20   95–483
ISBN 1–55661–505–1   CIP
                                                 AC

With love to my brother Don and my sister Karen who helped me catch our horse Silver even when they didn't want to. I am so fortunate to be in the same family as you.

LAURAINE SNELLING is a full-time writer who has authored a number of books, both fiction and nonfiction, as well as written articles for a wide range of magazines and weekly features for local newspapers. She also teaches writing courses and trains people in speaking skills. She and her husband, Wayne, have two grown children and make their home in California.

Her lifelong love of horses began at age five with a pony named Polly and continued with Silver, Kit, Rowdy, and her daughter's horse, Cimeron, which starred in her first children's book, *Tragedy on the Toutle*.

1

"ONE DAY—THE OLYMPICS."

Darla Jean Randall scrunched her eyes shut, crossed her fingers, and breathed her prayer all at the same time. She repeated it for good measure, then opened her green eyes and stared at the poster on the wall above her dresser. Five interlocking gold Olympic rings topped an illustration of a dark mahogany horse flying over a triple jump, its mane braided with red, white, and blue ribbons. The red-jacketed rider, in total control, rode poised over the horse's withers.

One day she would be in that picture. She, thirteen-year-old DJ Randall—well, fourteen minus twenty-one days—would hear the roar of the crowd as she and her mount triumphantly finished the cross-country course. When DJ closed her eyes again, she could almost feel the horse beneath her, the thrust of its powerful haunches sending them flying easily over the jumps. She could hear the cheers of the crowd, smell and taste the victory.

DJ reluctantly pulled her attention away from her daydream and clattered down the stairs. Her best friend, Amy Yamamoto, waited at the bottom.

"What took you so long?" Amy checked her watch.

"You've got a group lesson to teach in half an hour. And you know those little kids are chomping at the bit."

"Sorry. I got sidetracked." Darla Jean, known instead as DJ since she demanded everyone call her that, hopped on one foot while she pulled on a boot. She grabbed her riding helmet off the peg by the door, clapped it on her head, and instinctively tucked her wavy blond ponytail up into it.

"You be careful now." Her grandmother's voice followed her out the door.

"Yeah, I will." DJ's answer, yelled over her shoulder, was automatic.

The warm Pleasant Hill, California sun lay golden over the bleached tan hills of Briones Park to the west as DJ and Amy hopped onto their ten-speed bikes and pedaled up the slope.

"How do you plan to ride in the Olympics when you don't even have a horse?" Amy renewed the discussion they had had countless times before.

"Remember when I said I wanted to ride and you said I didn't even know how?"

"I know."

"I got a job at the Academy to pay for riding lessons, and everything worked out."

"Yeah, and how many gazillion stalls have we mucked out since then?"

DJ shifted down to pump up the steep hill ahead. "So now I need money to buy a horse of my own."

"You need to learn to jump first." Practical Amy, riding in front, had to yell to be heard.

"Sure would be super to be training my own horse at the same time." Labored puffs between DJ's words attested to the grade of the hill.

They crested the hill and coasted down the other side. Aluminum pipe fences surrounded the riding rings, open air stalls, and pasture area of Briones Riding Academy, known simply as the Academy by the working students and the others who rode there. A square white sign informed the public they could take lessons there and stable their horses.

The two girls turned into the gravel drive. "Too bad your mom can't buy you a horse."

"Right." DJ shrugged. "So what else is new? She couldn't afford lessons either, but I got 'em. I can't afford to wait around for her to help."

They parked their bikes in front of the low red barn with an aluminum roof. A raked sand aisle on each side divided the four lines of stalls fifteen box stalls long. Here lived the horses stabled at the Academy by outside owners. Some of them came to ride every day, but most of the animals were cared for and exercised by academy employees.

"I've got a treat for Diablo, then I'll meet you at the office." DJ dug in her pocket for the carrot pieces she always brought for the fiery sorrel gelding and trotted down the right aisle of stalls, calling out greetings to her favorite animals as she passed. She would have needed a bucket to treat all her friends.

"Hi, big fella," DJ grinned at the excited nicker from the restless sorrel. "I brought you something." Diablo lipped the carrot off her hand, rubbing his forehead against her chest while he munched. When he slobbered on her cheek, she inhaled a strong dose of carrot perfume. "You big silly. You act so tough, but you're really a marshmallow inside."

DJ rubbed the red's ears and murmured sweet words

all the while. She was sure she couldn't love him more if he really belonged to her. She buried her nose in his thick mane and breathed deep. Nothing in the entire world smelled as good as a horse.

Amy's whistle called DJ back to reality.

"See ya later." She tickled Diablo's whiskery lip one last time and headed back to the entrance, ignoring his pleading whinny.

"Looks like James didn't show up again," Amy said when DJ joined her. "The stalls need mucking, and I was supposed to do the show grooming today."

"We'll be here all afternoon." DJ's eyes lit up. "Extra money for lessons. Maybe there'll even be some to put in my horse fund!"

"Great. And I thought we could go swimming today." Amy propped both their bikes out of the way against the wall and stuck her hands in the back pockets of her jeans. "Come on, let's get going."

Dust puffed up around their boots as they walked across to the combination tackroom and office building. DJ lifted the clipboard with her class roster off the announcements wall and waved at Bridget Sommersby. Owner, trainer, boss, and good friend. Bridget sat working at her desk on the other side of the large square window.

Bridget signaled DJ to wait. "Angie's mother called. Angie caught a bug and won't be here today." She checked the calendar on her wall. "You're reviewing leads, right?"

"And starting figure eights. Shame Angie's missed so much. She's the only natural rider in the group."

"I know. Too bad kids with asthma seem to catch every bug that comes around. Angie's parents have signed her up for the next series of lessons, though. Say, DJ, after you are finished today, do you want to work Diablo? He needs extra attention. His owners called and said they would be out to see him."

"Really? I thought they'd forgotten all about him. Wish I could buy him." DJ shook her head. "Why own such a super horse and then never ride him?"

"Who cares? This way you can pretend he's yours." Amy picked up a bucket full of brushes and combs. "Where do you want me to start today, Bridget? That Quarter Horse's tail needs pulling if he's going to show. James should be here to help out. What happened to him *this* time?"

"I believe he is sick."

"Who called in his excuse, the nanny or the chauffeur?"

"Come on, now, don't be catty. It is not James' fault his father has as much money as the San Francisco mint."

"Well, he isn't learning much about responsibility when he only shows up when—"

"That is enough." Bridget didn't waste words any more than she wasted motions—or emotions for that matter. "I will come with you, Amy, so we can make some decisions." She ushered them out and closed the door behind her. "Oh, DJ, did you check with your grandmother about the show coming up? The entry fees should be sent in tomorrow."

DJ felt the familiar catch in her stomach. She *hated* asking Gran for money. But Mom was never around to ask. She was forever traveling for her job or at one of her graduate school courses. Not that she ever had money to give anyway.

"Yeah, I know. I gotta get to my class. Talk to you later." DJ strolled across the dusty parking lot to the front ring where two girls, ages eight and ten, stood by the gate with their horses' reins in hand.

"Okay, let's go over your gear." DJ spoke in the hearty, confident tone that helped make her a good teacher. No time now to think about money.

She carefully checked each girth, bit, and chin strap. When she had made sure the girls were wearing the required heeled boots, she swung open the gate. "Riders up."

DJ walked to the center of the deeply sanded ring and watched her charges walk their horses clockwise around its outer edge. Heads bobbing, the horses plodded along, well used to the routine. The girls sat deep in their saddles, heels down, eyes focused ahead on the spot between their horses' ears.

"Keep your right hand on your thigh," DJ called to one of the girls. "And don't let him go to sleep on you." After checking riders and horses again, she ordered a trot.

By the time the class was finished, DJ felt sweat beads trickling down her back.

"So how's the new saddle feel, Samantha? It must fit you better—you look more comfortable."

"I like it. It's still kinda stiff in the stirrups though."

"It will be for a while. A little saddle soap will help soften them up."

DJ motioned the other girl forward. "Krissie, you did real well today. Kept him off the rail and on a steady jog like I asked."

"He's a stubborn horse, but my mom says I'm stubborn enough for three people."

"Then the two of you should do just fine. If you could get out here to practice more, it would help."

"I know. Thanks for the lesson."

"You're welcome." DJ watched as her students headed for their stalls to put away their tack and brush down their mounts. Both owned their horses.

DJ ignored the tiny bite of jealousy she felt. *Beginning riders and they are already horse owners. What I wouldn't give*—she canceled the thought and followed her charges to the stables. Some of the academy riders' mothers waited patiently in their expensive, air-conditioned cars; others walked to the stalls to hurry their daughters along.

"DJ, when can our group go trail-riding in the Briones?" Samantha asked. Briones State Park bordered the west edge of the Academy's acreage.

"You guys have done so good! We'll pack lunches and go in two weeks. But, Sam, you need to get over here to practice more. You could be a really good rider if you did."

"I wish, but my mom is expecting a baby. She says she's too miserable to drive me over every day."

"So ride your bike."

The slender girl shook her head. "Too far. And Mom says the road's too dangerous." She scuffed her boot toe in the dust, studying the patterns she drew. "I want to be the best—you know, compete in the shows and stuff." She looked up at DJ, dark eyes serious. "Like you do."

DJ felt a curious knot in her middle. This could have been her at eight. Only her mom wouldn't have been pregnant. Of course, if her mom had ever found someone to marry, maybe there would have been a brother or sister for—DJ slammed the lid on those thoughts. She *never* let them out when other people were around.

"If you want it bad enough, you can make it happen." She knew where the words had come from. She hadn't planned on saying such a thing. But then, she hadn't planned on having this conversation either.

DJ grinned and tweaked Sam's red ponytail. She repeated her grandmother's words again, "If you want something bad enough, you can make it happen." Of course, Gran said to pray about it too, but DJ didn't think this was the right place to bring praying up. She ought to ask Gran out here to give the girls a pep talk, like a coach before a big game.

"You better get Soda brushed down, Sam. Your mom is waiting."

DJ joked with the girls while she supervised them caring for their horses. She did the heavy work—lifting the Western saddles down and standing them on their horns in the aisle—but each girl had to groom her own horse and take care of the stall and tack. While some people paid the Academy for these services, other parents felt that caring for a horse was part of ownership. DJ agreed.

She waved them both off, then walked back to the office. Maybe Bridget had time to talk now. Horses nickered for attention when she passed their stalls. She could hear Amy talking to someone over in the other aisle. It sounded like James had finally made it to work.

But when DJ got to the office, the academy owner was busy with another client, so she returned to the barns. There were still three stalls to muck out on this aisle before she could work with Diablo. She snapped the horses on the hot walker, cleaned the stalls, and spread new shavings in record time. Maybe she'd give

Diablo a bath after riding him.

DJ wiped the sweat off her face with the hem of her T-shirt. This July day was meeting its earlier promise of being warm to hot. She stopped at the drinking fountain on the north side of the stable and guzzled the tepid water before splashing some on her face. She'd make sure to splash plenty on herself while bathing the big red horse. The day was growing long. DJ wished she'd brought a lunch.

"Hi, fella, you miss me?" She stopped in front of the impatient gelding and slung her English saddle over the stall's half door. Diablo pawed the shavings down to the hard-packed dirt. He snorted, then pricked his ears forward. DJ stroked his long forelock and brushed it off the bright white diamond in the center of his forehead. A cowlick in the center swirled the hairs in a circle. "You're such a beauty. If only I could buy you. Wonder how much I'd need?"

He rubbed his forehead against her, leaving red and white hairs on her light purple T-shirt. DJ tickled the hairs sticking out of his ears. "Let's get going, you old silly." She kept up the easy murmur she used when working with the horses, talking to the sleek Thorough-bred-Quarter Horse cross as if he understood every word—and answered. Once he was bridled and saddled, she led him out to the cement block for mounting.

Today, just for today, she would pretend Diablo really *was* hers. After all, she *would* be showing him in less than two weeks. His owners, Mr. and Mrs. Ortega, seemed to appreciate how well she and Diablo were doing in the English Pleasure and the Trail Horse classes.

DJ spent the next hour and a half taking the gelding

through the entire routine for both classes. By the time they finished, both girl and horse wore a sheen of sweat.

"You two looked mighty good out there." Bridget met them at the gate and swung it open. "You have got him in top shape, both condition and training. Sure has improved since he came in."

"Do you think the Ortegas would like him to learn to jump?"

"I will ask. But seems to me *you* better learn first."

"I know. I want to so bad. How much would lessons cost?"

"Are you not earning enough right now? I have been waiting for you to ask. But you will need to start on old Megs. She knows the bars so well, she will be a good tutor for you."

DJ felt sure her face would split. She gave a decidedly unprofessional bounce in the saddle. Diablo threw his head up, and she tightened her grip on the reins. "Easy, boy, sorry about that. When can I start?"

Bridget smiled up at her star pupil. "Is tomorrow at eight all right? I know that is earlier than you usually come, but let us do it before the sun gets too hot." She slapped DJ on the knee and turned to leave. "Oh, I will ask the Ortegas tonight about jumping Diablo. You already have a good seat, so with some experience you could work with him."

DJ could almost see the Olympic rings shining on the wall of the building in front of her. She waved as Amy rode one of the stable horses into the ring. Amy preferred Western riding, so the two of them usually didn't compete in the same classes.

James followed on his dapple-gray Arab filly. DJ shook her head in disgust. If *she* had a horse like that, she'd sure find it easier to smile than he did.

If James had been one of her students, she would have told him to keep his back straight, his chin up, and his heels down. But he wasn't, and the last time she had made a suggestion—well, James had made it clear that he didn't take suggestions—or even orders—from *anyone*. When DJ had told Gran about the situation, she had said James really needed a friend.

"He can find someone else," DJ muttered, turning back to the barn. She could clean tack until Amy finished her lesson. Rubbing saddle soap into the leathers of a saddle required no brain power, leaving her mind free to explore the challenges of the Olympic long course. Cross country was the most difficult. She and Diablo would jump clean all the way around with the fastest time ever clocked. *First the triple jump, then the brush, then over a water jump . . .*

"You ready to go home or what?" The tone of Amy's voice indicated she'd asked the question before.

DJ jerked herself back to reality. The saddle she was soaping up had *some* shine to it.

Her pumping legs slowed when she pedaled from Amy's house to her own. Now she had to ask for money for the class entry fees. Maybe she should take it out of her horse account. But Gran had promised she would pay the entrance fees. All DJ had to do was ask.

DJ smiled. Why not require a signature in blood or a week of hard time digging in the backyard? Maybe she should offer to clean the kitchen every night without grumping. Not grumbling was the key. Even scrubbing toilets was better than doing dishes. DJ parked her bike carefully in the garage. Nothing fried her mother like something out of place.

Gran was so different from her mom. All Gran said to do was ask. She also told DJ to ask God when she needed something. DJ did remember to ask God for the most important things—at least some of the time. Like winning Olympic gold. It just didn't seem fair to bother God with the little things. She chewed on her thumbnail as she walked through the back door.

"Gran?"

"In the studio."

DJ padded through the living room and out to her grandmother's studio. In a normal family's home, it would have been the family room. Gran, a highly successful illustrator, stood in front of her easel, brush in hand and head cocked, studying her latest work.

"What do you think?"

DJ looked from the whimsical forest creatures dancing on the canvas to her grandmother dressed in matching hot pink shorts and tank top, both liberally decorated with bright dabs of paint. "The painting is awesome, like always, and you have yellow paint on your chin."

"No biggie." The artist stepped forward and applied two more brushstrokes to the fawn, bringing his spotted coat to life. "There, I'll leave it 'til tomorrow. I actually think it's done."

DJ sank into the stuffed rocker, her feet trailing over the arm. "Gran?"

"What, my darling?" The voice sounded vague, as if Gran were still off in the forest with her creatures.

DJ drew a circle around the puckered scar on her left

palm. The words wouldn't come. "When's Mom coming home?"

"Tomorrow night. Why?" Gran continued setting her paints in order. Other things might be left scattered around, but her paints and brushes were always cleaned and organized when she finished for the day.

"I need—ah—Gran, I need money for entry fees." The words stumbled over each other in their rush to reach air.

"Of course, why the hesitation? All you have to do is ask." Gran turned around, hands on her rounded hips. "How much do you need and by when?"

The whoosh leaving DJ's lungs set the folded paper swans attached to a twisted branch dancing on their threads. She named the amount.

"Check or cash?" Gran wiped the wisps of salt-and-pepper hair—heavy on the salt—back from her forehead. A puzzled look flitted across her face. "Did you have lunch? I don't think I did. What time is it anyway?" While she talked she dug in her huge satchel-style purse and pulled out a battered billfold. She wrote and handed DJ a check.

"I'll pay you back."

"You pay me back just by being yourself and helping when I ask. Working to pay for your own lessons is a big help. Besides, when was the last time I had to take out the garbage or mow and water the yard?" She threw her arm over DJ's shoulder and squeezed. "I just thank God I have money to give you."

DJ ducked her head, suddenly shy. That was her Gran all right. Always thankful for everything. But she *would* pay her back somehow.

Right after dinner, Gran buried her head in a book.

DJ climbed the stairs to her bedroom. This was the best time of day to draw. DJ's own pictures of horses filled her walls. Charcoal or pencil foals, Arabs, and jumpers surrounded the colored Olympic poster.

She piled her pillows against the headboard, propped her drawing board on her knees, and leaned back, waiting for inspiration to strike. Her pencil began to move as if controlled by some unseen force. Later, her drawing finished, she fell asleep with horses on her mind, the main one a fiery sorrel sporting a startling white diamond in the center of his forehead.

DJ rode out to the Academy by herself in the morning. Amy would be coming later. Her whistle set all the horses nickering as she jogged down the sandy aisle toward the red gelding's stall.

But Diablo didn't answer her whistle. His stall gate stood open, hooked to the side wall. All of his gear had been cleared out. Even the shavings had been swept away, leaving nothing but bare black dirt. DJ felt her happiness escape with a whoosh. Diablo was gone.

2

"BRIDGET! DIABLO'S MISSING!" DJ stopped to get her breath.

"Easy, girl." The trainer pushed her chair back from the desk. She checked the round clock on the wall. "I had hoped to see you before you . . ."

"But you don't understand. His stall is empty, even the shavings are gone. Did you move him?" The words tumbled over each other, picking up speed like rocks in a landslide.

"DJ, I know." Bridget pointed to one of the well-bruised chairs by her desk. "Sit."

"But . . ."

"Sit!" The command cracked through the stillness.

DJ did as ordered. She dug one chewed-off fingernail into the edge of her thumb. Visions of Diablo lying dead in the stall—or running away over the hills—raced through her mind.

"Now, I have bad news for you. You knew the Ortegas were coming last night to see Diablo?"

"Sure, I bathed him and everything so they would see I was taking good care of their horse." The desire to chew on her thumbnail made her raise her hand partway to her mouth. But, instead, she gripped one with the other and glued them to her knees.

"They came with a trailer and took him. They are moving and have a new stable lined up for him."

"Where did they go?" Instantly, her eyes burned. Her heart felt heavy. "Where did they take him?"

"Out of state. Texas, I think."

"So I won't ever see him again?" DJ couldn't have loved Diablo more if he'd been her own. How awful, not to see Diablo, not to ride him again, not to play with him in the corral.

Her shoulders slumped with the weight of the news. "Why didn't you warn me?"

Bridget shook her head. "I didn't know. Usually people give me thirty days notice—that's what our contract stipulates—but they just showed up. Said they had to move quickly, something about his job." She handed DJ an envelope. "Here, this is for you."

DJ took it and slid her finger under part of the flap. "Ouch." A paper cut opened a red line across the top of her finger. She finished opening the envelope and stuck her finger in her mouth to stop the bleeding. She looked up at Bridget, then dropped her gaze. The compassion in her mentor's eyes was too much for her to handle.

DJ pulled out a folded sheet of paper. Classic penmanship made it easy to read. *Dear DJ, please accept this token of our appreciation for the fine job you've done with Diablo. His conditioning and training show how much you've cared for him. We thank you and wish you the best in your endeavors. Sincerely, Manuel Ortega.* DJ unfolded the check.

"A hundred dollars." She stared at the zeros. Counted them again. "Look." She handed the check across the desk. "They gave me a hundred dollars."

"You earned every penny of it." Bridget handed it back with a smile. "That will help your horse fund."

DJ stuffed the note and check back into the envelope. "I was hoping to buy Diablo from them someday." The thought of never seeing her best friend again roared back.

Before DJ had more time to dwell on the bad news, Bridget pushed her chair back. "You better get Megs saddled and ready for your first jumping lesson. Our time is running out." She nodded toward the clock.

"Yes, ma'am." DJ jumped to her feet, stuffing the envelope in her pocket. "I'll be ready in ten."

She jogged across the dust-caked drive and back to the stables. Funny, the sun still shone and the birds sang. Maybe it was only her world that had stopped, not the one around her. Somewhere Diablo rode in a horse van, moving to his new home. Did he miss her as much as she already missed him?

She snagged a bucket with grooming gear, along with a jumping saddle and bridle, from the tack room and hustled down the long aisle. At least she didn't have to pass Diablo's empty stall. Megs, now retired from the show circuit but with a wealth of experience to teach her riders, hung her dark head out the stall door. She nickered when DJ came near, as did the other horses DJ ignored in her rush to ready the mare.

"Hi, girl." DJ hung the saddle and bridle on the half door hooked open to the wall, and slipped the mare a carrot piece. She grabbed a brush from the bucket, shoved the handle of the currycomb in her back pocket, and ducked under the web to begin the quickest grooming this side of tomorrow. Within minutes she had the mare brushed down and the tack in place. If one of her students had done that haphazard a job, she'd have made her redo it.

"I'll give you a really good brushing afterward," she promised as she led the Anglo-Arab bay mare down the aisle. "Then I'll turn you out for a while. How does that sound?" Megs clopped along beside her, ears pricked, head down as if hoping for a quick stroke now and then.

Once in the ring, DJ walked the mare around the outside, loosening her up even though they would be jumping only the lowest rails today. One thing Bridget drilled into her students and staff alike was that you could never be too careful with your horse. Not warming up enough led to strains and poor performance. A horse was like any other finely tuned athlete—warm muscles stretched easily and were less likely to suffer an injury.

DJ worked the mare through her paces: walk, trot, and collected canter. The thrill of riding a well-schooled horse sent DJ's mind instantly to the show-ring—and the Olympics. She jerked herself back to the present. If Bridget caught her daydreaming, she'd be grounded for sure.

Just as DJ was about to ask someone to fetch her instructor, Bridget entered the ring. She walked to each of the four jumps and checked the rails, all set at the lowest peg.

"Ready?"

"Yes, ma'am." DJ had watched enough classes and videos to know what was coming. She squeezed her lower legs to guide the mare over to the center of the ring. Even though she'd jumped before, this was her first official lesson.

"I hope you have not learned any bad habits that we

have to undo. Let me see you in your two-point trot, keeping the pace over the cavalletti." Bridget motioned to three parallel rails she had placed on the ground, spaced wide enough so the horse wouldn't stumble.

After DJ completed several successful rounds, Bridget moved to the center of the ring. "Good. Now, keeping the same pace, bring her over this jump. Remember to rest your weight in your heels and to lean into the jump. When you settle back, return to the two point."

Again, DJ did as asked, loving even the small moment of being airborne.

While DJ completed several circuits, Bridget lowered the rails on another jump and set the two in a straight line.

"Good, Megs. You're so smooth." DJ patted the mare's neck.

"Now maintain the pace up to the first obstacle, then canter to the next. Count the number of strides and keep her going straight."

Keep her between your hands and legs, DJ reminded herself. She had heard the instructions so many times before that she knew the routine, but making Megs do it exactly right wasn't as easy as she'd thought. Invariably Megs drifted to the right.

"Pay attention, DJ. You are using too much left leg."

DJ nodded but overcorrected, and Megs obediently swung to the right.

"You are trying too hard—just relax and forget we are in a class situation."

DJ tried to smile, but it felt more like a grimace. She set the mare into another round: cavalletti, two point, jump. Going straight was much harder than she'd ever dreamed.

"No, keep the pace. Get yourself in balance before you reach the jump."

DJ returned to the two point and completed the circle. Trot, jump, count one, two, three, four, five, and over. "Fiddle."

"What was wrong there?"

"I needed six strides and I used five."

"And got left behind?"

DJ nodded. Circle again. Jump, count, and jump. By the end of the hour, DJ could feel the pull in both her back and calves.

"You must keep her going straight. She has a tendency to pull to the left."

"I know. I'm using too much right leg."

"I know you know, so don't let her. One more time around and we will call it a day."

DJ concentrated on everything she'd been told. This time Megs jumped once, took six strides at a canter, made another jump, and headed straight toward the arena fence before dropping back to the trot. DJ rode a tight circle and met Bridget at the gate.

"I have always said you have a good seat," Bridget commented when DJ stopped in front of her. "I know you would practice for hours if you could. Just do not neglect your other duties. You know which horses need the work. I will lay out a program for you if you like."

"Thank you. Oh, thank you, Bridget! I can't wait to try the big ones." Visions of triple jumps, water jumps, brush jumps, and in-and-outs flew through her mind.

"In good time." Bridget shared one of her rare smiles with her charge. "Now, you have stalls to clean and horses to work—after you cool out Megs, of course. Oh, and about the show. You know you may ride one of the school horses."

DJ's shoulders slumped. No Diablo to show meant no chance for a decent ribbon. She mentally ran through the stable horses. Only Megs would have a chance, and she was retired. Bridget would never change her mind on that.

"Thanks, but none of them are ready. I'll help coach the beginners." The thought of not competing in the better classes this summer made her groan. If only she had a horse of her own—then things like this wouldn't happen. Now she had to prepare another horse, which also wouldn't be her own. She clenched her teeth as a blaze of anger ripped through her.

Megs jigged to the side. "Sorry, girl." DJ ordered her body to relax. *There must be a connection between my knees and my jaw.*

She looked up to catch a look from Bridget that clearly said, never take your personal problems out on your horse.

"I'm sorry." DJ seemed to be saying that a lot. "I . . . I . . . what if I can't show at all this summer?"

"Is that what is worrying you?" Bridget stepped close to Megs' shoulder. "There will always be a horse here for you to ride. You just need to take the time to prepare one. I will talk with one of the owners. Mrs. Orlando might be pleased to have you show one of her horses."

DJ started to ask which one, but thought the better of it. Early on she'd learned that when Bridget was ready to tell her something, she would. And asking before that would not make her popular with the academy owner.

"Someday I'll have a horse of my own."

"Yes, I am sure you will." Bridget laid a hand on DJ's knee. "I *know* you will. Now, take care of the ones you can." She patted Megs' neck and walked out of the gate. Two people were waiting to talk with her outside the arena.

Feeling as if she were floating on a cloud, DJ nudged the mare into a trot. She had plenty of work to do.

Along with each shovelful of shavings and manure, she tossed out another moneymaking idea. She *had* to buy a horse of her own. But first she had to earn the money. Counting the check this morning, her total now stood at $189.89. If only she didn't have to buy things like presents and give part of her earnings to Sunday school.

"I'm never going to a movie again," she muttered, spreading the clean shavings she'd hauled in.

"What's up?" Amy stopped with her wheelbarrow.

"The Ortegas moved away and took Diablo with them."

"That's why his stall is empty?"

"Yup. At least now I don't have to spend Gran's money for entry fees. I won't be showing."

"Not ever?"

"Don't be dumb." DJ leaned on her pitchfork. "Bridget says I can use school horses to show, but none of them are ready for Saturday."

"You can use Josh." Amy offered her most prized possession.

"Ames, you know that won't work. Our classes are usually at the same time—besides, I've never ridden him in competition." She looked deep into her friend's eyes. "You're the best. Thanks."

"James isn't here—again." Amy rolled her eyes. "I've

had to do most of his work."

"Again? What's with him anyway?"

"Wish I knew." Amy picked up the handles of the barrow. "Gotta finish so I can work Josh. Hey, how did your lesson go?"

"Great. I was born to jump, I just know it." DJ closed her eyes and saw five interlocking rings on the back of her eyelids. She crossed her fingers and breathed her prayer. *Someday, the Olympics.*

"Ames, I *have* to find some ways to earn money this summer. You had any brilliant ideas lately?"

"Sorry." Amy shrugged and trundled her wheelbarrow down the aisle.

That evening when her mother returned home from her latest business trip, DJ had just finished setting the table.

"Darla Jean, how many times have I asked you to put your bike away? One of these days I'm going to run over it, and then where will you be?" Lindy Randall dropped her briefcase on a chair and crossed to the sink to pour herself a glass of water.

DJ clenched her teeth. She'd been so anxious to tell Gran the bad news, she'd forgotten her bike. Fiddle. She slammed the napkins down on the table and headed for the garage. Now she didn't dare mention needing extra money for her horse fund. Double fiddle.

3

"DJ, I'M SORRY. I DIDN'T MEAN TO SCOLD YOU first thing." Lindy stood in the doorway to DJ's room. She had changed out of her business suit and into an emerald lounging outfit.

"I know. It was my fault. I couldn't wait to tell Gran about Diablo." DJ looked up from her drawing. "You look nice." Her mother always looked stylish, dressed in the latest fashion. DJ looked down at her tanned legs topped by the cutoffs she'd put on after her return from the stable. Jeans or shorts and T-shirts—what else did a kid need anyway? Besides her outfits for competition, of course, and Gran made most of those.

"Thanks, can I come in?"

"Sure." Her mother's recent insistence on privacy—both her own and her daughter's—still caught DJ by surprise sometimes.

Lindy looked down at her daughter's drawing of a jumping Thoroughbred. "You're getting to be very good at that, you know. I'm glad one of us got Mother's talent." She sat down on the end of the bed. DJ watched her mother pleat the fabric of her pants. Something was up. But what?

Lindy looked up, her chin-length hair swinging as she moved her head. "What happened with Diablo?"

"They . . . the Ortegas moved to Texas and took him away."

"Without telling you?"

"Even Bridget didn't know. And now I don't have a horse to compete with this summer." DJ wanted to go on to say that if her mother spent less money on clothes, she might have some cash to buy her daughter a horse, but she didn't. She'd heard the argument too many times: "Fashionable clothes help make sales, and if I don't make sales, we don't eat."

"I'm sorry. I wish I could help, but right now my company is talking about cutting back. What little I have saved might have to tide us over if I get laid off."

"You've been their best rep for the last two years, Mom. Why would they let you go?" When would her mother think of something besides her job and getting her next degree? DJ had a whole slew of questions that she kept hidden in a box in her mind. A box labeled *Mother*.

"Well, when I get my Masters of Business Administration, they'll have to take notice. If they don't, I'll find a better job." She nodded as if to convince herself. "So I better get to studying."

"So what's new?" DJ mumbled in spite of her promise to herself not to be a smart mouth.

"Darla Jean, I'm doing this as much for you as for me."

"Right. Sorry." There, she'd done it again. Why couldn't they just talk like Amy and her mother did? Instead, she couldn't keep from giving a smart answer every time her mom said something.

"Well, I am doing this for you. And a little gratitude might go a long way." Lindy flounced out of the room, leaving a trail of expensive perfume.

DJ heaved a sigh and set her sketch pad down on the double bed. This certainly hadn't been one of her better days. She uncrossed her legs and slid to the edge of the bed. Gran would remind her that her mother was under a great deal of pressure. That selling equipment such as guns and flak vests to police departments and sheriffs' offices was usually a man's job. That her mother felt the need to be so much better than the male sales representatives in order to keep her position.

DJ had heard the story too many times to count. She tried to remember the last time her mother had made it to one of *her* events. Her mom had missed the horse shows, the art fair at school—even missed her thirteenth birthday.

DJ trailed a hand on the banister on her way down to Gran's sun-room that extended from the family room. She knew she'd find her grandmother curled up in her tattered but comfortable wing chair. She'd be reading a mystery, her favorite kind of book. Or else writing a letter. Gran was great about writing letters to her two sisters who still lived where they grew up in Georgia.

But Gran wasn't in her chair. She wasn't hiding behind an easel, sneaking in some extra work hours. She wasn't in the kitchen making their favorite snack—popcorn, slathered with butter.

"Gran?" DJ checked the laundry room and glanced out at the deck.

Coming back through the French doors, she heard the murmur of voices from her mother's room. DJ grabbed an apple out of the bowl on the kitchen counter and ambled up the stairs. She started to tap on the almost-closed door to her mother's room but stopped.

"But I just don't know what to say to her." Lindy sounded depressed.

"She took the news of losing Diablo pretty hard."

"Oh really? She barely mentioned it. She never talks to me, unless it's a smart remark. Was this the way I was at her age?"

A soft chuckle. "No, you were much worse. You were boy crazy by twelve."

"Yeah, and look what it got me."

DJ couldn't hear Gran's answer.

"At least boys aren't a problem—are they?" A pause. "Oh, Mother, I don't know how you stood it."

"The good Lord's grace, that's how. You might find it, too, if you asked."

"I don't need you preaching to me." The tone switched to harsh resentment.

"You asked, I told you. Now about you and DJ . . ."

DJ leaned closer, but the voices dropped to a low murmur. Gran always said that eavesdroppers heard only bad things about themselves. *Ha!* She shrugged. Who knew when stored information could be useful? Another shrug, this one forced. It sure would be helpful if she and her mother could really talk for a change. Then she wouldn't have to go around feeling guilty so often.

DJ meandered back down to the kitchen, tossing her apple core in the compost bin. She and Gran recycled everything possible. Just last week DJ had turned in aluminum cans and made three dollars, all in nickels. But then a dollar was a dollar no matter what form it came in. She stashed it all in her horse box. Every time she reached $10, she made a bank deposit.

She stuck her head in the refrigerator. Nothing to munch, unless you counted the bag of carrots her mother kept. Horse treats. She checked the cupboard. Microwave popcorn, nothing like the kind Gran made from scratch. She pulled a bag from the box.

"I made popcorn if anybody wants some," she yelled up the stairs on her way to the family room and the television set. When nothing caught her interest and no one came to share her popcorn, she dragged her feet back up the stairs to her room.

What a crummy ending to a perfectly crummy day. Other than her lesson, she corrected. The thought of jumping helped her pick up her feet until she entered her room. The 8 x 10 photo Amy had taken of her and Diablo in the ring last summer sent her spiraling again.

She banished the threat of tears with a clamped jaw. Crying was for babies. She ripped the half-finished picture of the jumper off the pad, crumpled it between both hands, and stuffed it in the wastebasket. It wasn't good enough anyway. Something was wrong with the thrust of the back legs.

If she only had a horse of her own, everything would be all right.

Morning dawned along with the beginnings of a moneymaking idea. DJ flew to the window and gazed out at the backyard. The hummingbirds were already buzzing. House finches sang at the seed feeders and two bright yellow and black goldfinches hung upside down on the thistle feeder. DJ sucked in a breath of crisp morning air, flavored with the scent of the roses that bloomed around the deck below her second-floor window.

This had to be a better day than yesterday. If she hurried, maybe she could get in an hour on Megs before she had to start her chores. She tugged a brush through her long blond hair while she pelted down the stairs. Her mother would already have left for work, so she didn't have to worry about making conversation.

"You have to eat before you leave," Gran called from her chair. As usual, she sat curled with her steaming mug of coffee on the table beside her and her Bible in her lap.

DJ crossed the room to drop a kiss on her tumbled hair. "I will. You want something?"

"I'll make scrambled eggs if you wait long enough."

"No, I can eat a food bar on the way." DJ headed back to the kitchen. "How come we're out of fruit?"

"You ate it all."

DJ sneaked the orange juice container out and began chugging from the pour spout.

"Darla Jean Randall, you pour that into a glass."

DJ flinched and shoved the jug back in the fridge. Taking out the milk, she did as Gran asked. Drinking from the container was certainly much quicker.

"Will you call Amy and tell her I already left?" She returned from the open door and grabbed a second food bar for her pocket. That would be a morning snack.

"Please? Tell her I left for the Academy at"—she checked her watch—"six-thirty, and she should get her b—"

"Darla Jean! Ladies don't use words like that."

"Sorry, Gran. See ya." DJ let a grin stretch her cheeks.

What would Gran do if her darling granddaughter ever said a *really* bad word? Like some of the four-letter words she heard every day at school? One thing Gran liked about Bridget, she didn't tolerate swearing either.

DJ pedaled by Amy's house, wishing she could have called. But Mrs. Yamamoto had made it clear that no calls were tolerated before seven-thirty in the morning or after nine at night. And it wasn't even seven yet.

Was her idea a good one? Could she and Amy pull it off? Would it make enough money for her so she could buy a horse by summer's end?

The hour in the ring with Megs flew faster than they took the jumps. *Squeeze. Lift. Let Megs show you how to judge the distances; she's an expert. Use your knees.* All the commands of the day before echoed in her head. She'd heard them before, but it was different when they were directed at her.

Oh, the feeling of flying! The thrust of powerful hindquarters and then . . . for that brief second, to be free. And these were only small jumps. What must the larger ones feel like?

"Look straight ahead, between her ears," Bridget called from the fence. "That is right. Do not rush. The more relaxed you are, the more comfortable your mount will be."

DJ completed another circuit and rode over to the fence. "You seen Amy yet?"

"No. By the way, James' housekeeper called. He will be in today—"

DJ snorted in what Gran would call a decidedly unladylike manner.

Bridget cut her a glance that said she entirely agreed with Gran. She continued as if there had been no interruption. "—and he will clean one extra row of stalls, down to the dirt."

DJ knew James was getting punished.

"*And* he will spend two hours cleaning tack. Then he will work in the ring for an hour. I do not want to hear about any comments from you and Amy."

That James! On top of leaving most of his work to the other staff, he was a whiner and a tattletale. What she wouldn't like to do to him!

"Understood?"

Why did Bridget stick up for him? She and Amy knew the instructor never played favorites. James deserved a good yelling at. He even neglected his own horse. *If I had a horse like Gray Bar, I'd spend every minute of my life with her.*

DJ quit studying her hands and looked at Bridget. "Understood." She leaned forward and stroked the bay mare's neck. "I better cool her out." She turned Megs back to the ring. They'd walk around twice, and then she'd put the bay on the hot walker so she could muck stalls.

One thing was sure, there was never a lack of work to do around the Academy. Maybe her other dream of someday owning one wasn't such a hot idea after all.

Amy's entrance snapped DJ out of her daydreams. "Hey, thought you were going to sleep all day."

"I called at seven and you'd already left. Why didn't you tell me you were going so early?"

"I didn't know. I just woke up and couldn't wait to get here. Besides, you know your mom says no early calls. But hurry with your stalls, I got a great idea!"

"What?"

"Can't tell you now. But it's a hummer." DJ grinned

at the look on Amy's face. Her dark almond-shaped eyes nearly disappeared when Amy glared. And she was definitely glaring.

"You know I hate secrets." Amy planted both fists on her nearly nonexistent hips. Their flat-chested bodies were one of their big-time gripes.

"I know." DJ attacked her stall with a vengeance.

At the water hose an hour later, DJ ran some over her neck and up her arms.

"Okay, what's your idea?" Amy grabbed the hose and mimicked her friend's actions.

"First, look at me." Amy did. "Do I look green-eyed to you?"

"Silly, you always look green-eyed. You *have* green eyes."

"No, I mean the green-eyed monster—you know—jealousy."

"Who would you be jealous of?"

"James."

"James? Why?"

"His horse. What I wouldn't do for a registered Arab like Gray Bar, and he doesn't even take good care of her."

Amy turned off the faucet. "No, you aren't bitten by the monster. But you're going to be murdered by another one—namely me—if you don't tell me what your idea is."

"Pony rides at birthday parties!"

"What in the world are you talking about? We don't even have a pony."

"You want to hear more or not?"

4

"DUMB QUESTION. WHAT ARE YOU DREAMING up now?"

"You know I need money to buy a horse. You also know we need to exercise Bandit. Right?"

"Yeah, his family almost never comes." Amy turned the hose back on for a drink.

"And you like to take pictures."

"I don't just take pictures. I'm a photographer." The glint in her eye warned DJ to tread lightly. "Or will be someday."

"Your family just got a new Polaroid camera, right?" Teasing Amy like this was a privilege given only to best friends.

Amy flicked the hose, sending drops of water at DJ. "If you don't get to the point, you'll get soaked."

"Do I have to draw you a map?" DJ ducked, but her T-shirt darkened with wet blotches anyway.

"All right, come on." DJ sank down on a concrete block against the barn wall and patted the block beside her. "Sit."

Once they were both leaning elbows on knees, she turned so she could watch Amy's face. "The way I see it, we both want and need money this summer—me for a horse, and you for film, so . . ." She paused for dramatic effect. "So we ask the McDougalls if we can use Bandit to entertain kids at birthday parties. The kids get to ride a pony we lead, have their pictures taken in a Western hat on the pony, and the adult in charge pays us. See, with the Polaroid they can take their pictures home with them." By the end of her speech, DJ bounced up from her block and began pacing in front of Amy, arms waving for emphasis.

She stopped. Planted her hands on her hips. Waited. "Well?"

"I'm thinking."

"I can tell." DJ started to say something else but caught herself. Amy always needed thinking time.

"We don't have a pony, a hat, customers, or a camera. We've never done anything like this. How do we let people know about it?" She closed her eyes as if to concentrate better. "And . . . how much would we charge?"

With the final question, DJ knew Amy planned to go along with the idea.

"Super, huh?"

"Yeah, if we can work it all out. I'll ask my dad about using the camera. Maybe he'll have some suggestions for us."

"And I'll ask Bridget for the McDougalls' phone number and call them. My mom knows a lot about selling stuff, so I'll"—she stopped her pacing to point at Amy—"*we'll* talk to her together. That way she won't think this is another of my 'harebrained schemes'—her words."

"You gotta admit you've come up with some wild ones."

"It wasn't my fault the Great Dane got away. How was

I to know he didn't understand leash laws?"

"What about breeding hamsters?"

"So they chewed a hole in their box. That guy with the snake was glad to take the ones that didn't get away."

"Snails?"

"They said the restaurants would pay thirty-five cents each. Anyway, the book said to feed them cornmeal; I thought they'd like it."

"Yeah, well, they liked your grandmother's garden better."

"That was still a good idea. If we ever do it again, I figured out how to make a box even a snail couldn't escape."

"And what about selling greeting cards?"

DJ sank down on the block. "So we've tried different stuff. We *did* make some money selling fruit and vegetables door to door."

"Sure, after your grandma grounded us for a week for picking her strawberries without asking."

"I thought she was done making jam."

"Well, one thing we've learned—or at least *I've* learned—you've got to think things through. Ask lots of questions. This time we don't just jump in and . . ."

"I could draw a real neat cartoon for some fliers. We could use it on invitations and . . ."

Amy shook both her head and her friend.

But DJ was off and running. Like a filly with the bit in her teeth, she took off toward the office. "I'll talk to Bridget right now," she called back from halfway across the parking lot. "We'll have a zinger of a time."

"Hey, Cat Eyes, the bogeyman chasing you?"

The voice stopped DJ in her tracks. *James.* Where had he come from? She turned and looked toward the sound. Sure enough, there he stood in the barn door. The little creep. Life around the Academy was so much sweeter when he didn't show up, even though they had to do all his work.

She turned back toward the office. Maybe if she ignored him, he'd go away. She heard a snicker from behind the line of cars. Sure enough, James must have brought a friend along. He always played best to an audience.

"As if anyone would really be his friend." Her mutter carried her into the dark of the building. She blinked in the dimness, but it didn't slow her pace. If only Bridget had a minute right now!

But the office was empty. DJ checked the board. No classes scheduled. Where was Bridget? Should she flip through the file and find the McDougalls' number herself? She gnawed the end of her already chewed-to-the-quick thumbnail.

"Fiddle. Double fiddle." She swung around and charged out the door, nearly colliding with Bridget as she walked in. "Bridget, I got an idea."

"Thank the Lord for small favors." The woman's grin made sure there was no sting in her words. "Just leave me standing vertical, I listen better in an upright position."

"Sorry. Amy and I are gonna give pony rides at birthday parties so we can earn extra money, so can you give me the McDougalls' phone number so I can call them to see if they'll loan me Bandit?" DJ ran out of air.

"Glad you have to breathe occasionally." Bridget crossed the room to her desk.

"We'll take pictures of the kids on the pony with the Polaroid camera . . ."

"Hold it." Bridget pointed at the chair beside the desk. "Let me think a minute."

DJ perched on the edge of the chair. She hastily stuck her hands between her knees so she wouldn't chew her nails. Bridget did not like to see her students chewing their fingernails. She said it didn't look professional.

"I will give you their number on one condition. You give me a signed paper saying your mom approves and accepts responsibility."

DJ could feel her excitement drain out the toes of her boots. "But . . ."

"No *buts*. You are a hard worker and a responsible girl, but you do go off half-cocked sometimes with new ideas. Since Bandit is stabled here, I have to make sure my clients are cared for properly."

"We wouldn't hurt Bandit." The thought that Bridget could think she wouldn't take good care of a horse made DJ's heart pound.

"DJ, I know that. But you cannot control everything around you. Learning to look at all sides of something and making good plans is part of growing up and becoming an adult. I know how bad you want a horse, so I will help you all I can—but I need to cover myself, too. Bring me the signed paper, then you can call them. I will put in a good word for you if they ask."

DJ nodded. "Okay. Thank you." She got to her feet. The ideas that had been swirling and jumping in her brain now lined up with some sense to them. She had to get her mother's permission. Not Gran's, her mother's. It seemed impossible.

5

"MOM'S HOME. CAN YOU COME OVER?" DJ spoke softly into the phone so no one would hear her.

"I'll ask." DJ heard the phone clunk on the counter and noises in the background. With four kids in the family, there was always noise at the Yamamotos'. "Yes, I can. You want me to bring the stuff?"

The two of them had spent the afternoon making lists and writing plans so they could present their ideas in a businesslike way. Both Lindy and Mr. Yamamoto would appreciate that.

"Have you talked with your mom and dad yet?" DJ twirled the cord around her finger.

"No, we said to wait."

"I know, but . . ." Leave it to Amy. She always did exactly as they agreed. DJ had told Gran all about the idea as soon as she got home. Gran said she'd hold judgment until after the conference. But DJ could tell by the twinkle in her grandmother's eye that she approved. As usual, Gran said, "I'll pray we'll be doing what is in God's will for us."

DJ wished she'd have thought of that without the reminder.

"Mom." DJ knocked on her mother's bedroom door. "Can Amy and I talk with you?"

"Sure." Lindy came to the door, pushing her glasses up on her head. "Up here or down in the family room?"

"Well, I'd kinda like Gran in on it, too."

"Okay, give me a sec to save what's on the computer. Fix us some iced tea, all right?"

DJ and Amy pounded down the carpeted stairs. Within minutes they had four tall glasses of raspberry iced tea on a tray. "Grab some cookies." DJ pointed at the sunflower cookie jar. "Gran baked today."

With the treats served, DJ didn't know what to do with her hands. Other than eat and drink.

"So?" Lindy tucked her legs up under her.

DJ started to chew her fingernail but stopped herself. Her mother looked like someone right off a magazine page, and here DJ was still in her shorts. At least she didn't have jeans on. Her mother didn't think horse scent made a good perfume.

She and Amy swapped looks. Amy's clearly said, "Get going."

"Mom, we have an idea . . . a business idea, and . . ." Once she got started, the words rushed like a creek after a winter rain. When she forgot something, Amy filled in. They spread their papers out on the floor and explained each detail.

When her mother joined the girls on the floor and started asking questions, DJ began to hope.

"How about if I buy the Western hat and give you a loan for the printing costs?" Lindy marked some numbers on one of the sheets of paper. Her glasses had migrated back down on her nose.

DJ knew they were home free. Now to get permission to use Bandit.

"What do your parents say, Amy?" Lindy turned to the girl beside her.

"We haven't asked them yet."

"We thought we'd start here," DJ chimed in.

Lindy tapped her chin with the end of a pen. "This can't be run like your other 'businesses.'" The look in her eye said she remembered the hamsters and their progeny. She never had cared for "creepy crawly things," as she referred to them. Along with a few other words and in a more than slightly raised tone of voice.

"We're older now . . ."

"And more responsible." The two girls ran their sentences together. That happened a lot with them.

"I would like to help design the fliers." Gran slid from her chair to join the others on the floor. "And I have a friend who would give you a good price on the printing."

"Now for the important question. Do you know any parents who have kids with summer birthdays?"

"You do." Amy stuck her tongue in her cheek.

DJ gave her one of *those* looks.

"Surely there will be some at church. I'll check." Gran wrote herself a note.

"But the parties have to be within walking distance. We don't have a trailer or anything." Amy leaned her elbows on her crossed legs. "I guess the next thing is for me—for us—to ask my mom and dad. We need to write up a paper . . ."

"An agreement," Lindy put in.

"We'll all sign it and turn it in to Bridget," DJ finished.

"This is gonna take forever." She lay back on the carpet. "Besides all this, we still have no idea how much to charge." She flopped her hands over her head so the backs slapped the floor.

"You showed me a partial cost sheet," Lindy said while searching through the scattered papers. "Here. It'll be about . . ." She neatly penciled numbers beside the items they'd have to purchase. "Now, add them up and divide by—how many parties do you think you can do this summer? One a week, two?"

The girls looked at each other and shrugged. "Many as we can get, I guess."

"No, let's say twelve to start with. See, divide your total by twelve." She handed the sheet back to the girls. "Okay, now that gives you the cost of the party. Whatever you set above that is your profit."

By the time they'd finished, they had an agreement, a budget, a simple business plan, and aching heads.

By the next evening they had the Yamamotos' permission and a phone number for the McDougalls. An answering machine picked up the call.

"Fiddle!" DJ let the phone clatter into the cradle. Amy, upstairs on the extension, sighed as she came down the stairs. Clattering wasn't her style.

"So what did they say?" Gran asked from her chair. She pushed her glasses back up on her nose.

"Answering machine." The two girls sank to the floor at Gran's knees.

"Have you prayed about this venture of yours?"

Both nodded their heads.

"Good. Then if it's supposed to happen . . ."

"The doors will open." Again the two spoke in unison. They couldn't count high enough to number the times they'd heard those words.

Gran grinned and laid a hand on each head. "You've listened well."

"The phone!" Amy and DJ leaped to their feet and charged for the kitchen. When an unfamiliar voice asked to speak with DJ, her heart started beating triple-time.

"Speaking."

"Hi, you called me? I know you, don't I, from the Academy?"

DJ mumbled a response. Amy glared at her. DJ took a deep breath and started again. "Yes, my friend Amy Yamamoto and I take care of Bandit. And that's what we'd like to talk to you about. You see, we would like to earn some money this summer . . ." As she went on to explain their idea, Amy ran back upstairs to listen on the extension.

"What does Bridget think of this?" Mr. McDougall asked.

"She said she'd call and talk with you if you'd like."

"She thinks it's a good idea," Amy added.

"Let me talk this over with my wife—it's really her pony. We'll call you back in a few minutes."

Amy charged back down the stairs. The two of them fished cans of soda from the refrigerator and plunked down by the phone.

"You think they'll say yes?" Amy sipped from her can.

"I hope." DJ checked the clock again. Five minutes! It seemed more like fifteen.

"Your dad sure was nice about us using the camera."

"I know."

The phone rang. The girls looked at each other. It rang again.

"Here goes everything." DJ picked up the receiver.

6

"YOU WILL? WE CAN! OH YES, WE'LL TAKE THE best care of Bandit in the whole world." DJ could hardly keep her feet on the floor.

"But there's one catch. We'd like you to do a party for our five-year-old son, Danny. Without charge, of course."

"Of course." DJ hoped she sounded like a businesswoman. "And what will you charge us for the use of Bandit?" She hoped Amy was impressed.

"Why nothing—the party, that's it."

DJ swallowed a shriek. "Th-thank you. We'll be talking with you later, about the party I mean." She hoped she got all the words in the right order, but she wasn't sure.

"Kiddy parties, here we come!" The two danced around the kitchen, ducking and spinning like Indian braves.

Amy froze in the middle of the floor. "What are we gonna call our business?"

"Pony Parties, of course." DJ danced on. "But will people think we're bringing a bunch of ponies?"

"We'll tell 'em up front. Besides, our flier will say . . ."

DJ froze beside Amy. "We better get going on our flier." The two headed for DJ's bedroom, grabbing a sack of pretzels on the way.

DJ was nearly asleep that night when another good idea came creeping out of the mist and bit her. Long ago she'd adopted her grandmother's habit of keeping a notebook and pencil by her bed to capture good ideas. She'd learned the best ideas came right before sleep and just before she opened her eyes in the morning. "Offer Western or English pony parties," she muttered as she wrote. She studied the page. Maybe it wasn't such a good idea. She flipped off the light and snuggled back under the covers.

But now her mind wouldn't shut down. Instead, it traveled back to the session with her mother and Gran. Gran could always be counted on to pitch in with a new project, but not her mother. She'd never seen her mother in business action before. If she was this way at work, it was no wonder she usually made top salesperson for the company.

So how come she can never find time to be with me? DJ let the thought peek out of the internal box where she kept things that hurt too much to think about. *Maybe if I wore dresses sometimes* . . . The thought made her gag. *I do look pretty good when I'm dressed for a show.* She had to believe that. Bridget said as much and she never gave out compliments just to give them out.

It's just me. I know it is. I leave things around, and I can't help the smart mouth. The words leap out before I can stop them. It's probably even my fault my father left. Images floated through her mind. There weren't any of her father. Most of her memories were of her and Gran.

She didn't remember much about Grandpa, either. He died when she was four.

"Dear God, I'm sorry for all the stuff I do wrong. Thank you for Gran and for Mom. Help me to do my best. Amen." She flipped over to her other side. Maybe *now* she could go to sleep. "Oh, and, God, please take care of Diablo—wherever he is."

Each day the empty stall reminded her again of Diablo. Where was he? How was he? Was anyone exercising him? Did they give him carrots and brush his flanks carefully? He was so ticklish!

That afternoon when she finally got home, she fixed herself a sandwich and took it in to watch Gran paint.

"Hi, dear. Say, that looks good. Would you mind fixing one for me?"

"You haven't eaten? It's after three." DJ bit her tongue before she said what she thought. Gran forgot all about eating or anything else when the "creative genius," as she called it, took over.

Gran flinched. "I know, I know better. But I lost track of time."

"I'll fix yours. You want mayo or mustard?" DJ threw the questions over her shoulder on the way back to the kitchen.

"Mayo if it's tuna; mustard with baloney."

When DJ got back, Gran stood in front of the easel studying the forest scene she was painting. "That's a new one. I like the trees."

"Umm." Gran took the plate DJ offered without taking her eyes from the easel. "It needs more depth. I want the reader to feel as if they can't resist that path any more than Tara can." She crossed the room to her wing chair and nestled into it. Tara was the name of the character in the book she was illustrating.

DJ still stood in front of the painting. "Makes me want to go there."

"Darlin', 'go' is your middle name. But thanks for the compliment. So how'd you do this morning?" She took a bite of her tuna. "Who taught you to make such good sandwiches?"

DJ grinned at her. "You did."

"Really?" Gran studied the bread. "But then you do all kinds of things well. Have I told you lately how proud I am of you?"

"Thanks, Gran, I needed that." She started on the second half of her sandwich, trying not to talk with her mouth full but wanting to catch Gran up on everything that had happened. When she told about James calling her "cat eyes," Gran shook her head, sending the tendrils of hair around her face to swinging. "That poor boy. Mark my words, something tragic is going to happen there."

"Yeah, I might pound him into the dust one of these days."

"No you won't. You'll keep on praying for him like we said . . ."

"*You* said," DJ muttered.

"Like we agreed." Gran sent her one of those smiles that made it impossible to argue.

"But if I had a horse like his, I'd . . ."

"Now, child, a horse isn't everything. We'll keep on praying." She leaned forward and tapped the end of DJ's nose. "And I'll pray especially that you can find it in your heart to be kind to James."

DJ groaned. When her grandmother started to seriously pray about something—look out! DJ finished her sandwich and picked up the crumbs with a wet fingertip. "Gran, do you still miss Grandpa sometimes?"

"More than just sometimes, but nothing like I used to. There comes a day when you find yourself remembering something really good, maybe a fun time, with that person. Then it doesn't hurt so much. It takes time, of course."

"I wish it didn't. I sure miss Diablo."

By the end of the next week, with DJ's birthday only three days away, Bridget had the rails up two more notches when DJ came for her lesson. She worked Megs around the edge of the ring, careful to warm the mare up even though she couldn't wait to get going. Post to the trot, collected canter—the horse responded smoothly to DJ's lower leg and hand signals. Megs knew the drill inside and out and seemed to be having as much fun as her rider. Ears pricked and with an occasional snort, she went through her paces.

"All right, take the two low ones on the outside first, then head up the middle for the others." Bridget had taken her place in the center of the ring, the best place to watch for each flaw of DJ's performance.

"No, do not let her rush it. You are signaling her to lift off too soon. A good rider is a calm rider. Now, again."

DJ tried to keep her excitement under her hat, but it wasn't easy. After the next round, Bridget signaled her over.

"Keep your hands like so, and your knees here." With

each command she put DJ in the proper position. "Now, again."

By the end of the session, DJ didn't want to hear "now, again" for a long time. One thing about Bridget, you had to have one skill down perfectly before you could go on to the next.

"Okay, work on those the next few days. Remember to picture the perfect jump in your head. See yourself doing it perfectly every time. It is not practice that makes perfect, but perfect practice that makes perfect."

DJ said the same to her young students at the class she taught an hour later. *Perfect practice*—she'd remember that one.

"When are we going on our ride up into the park?" Sam asked at the end of the session.

"You promised," Krissie chimed in.

DJ pretended to be deep in thought. "You really think you can handle your horses well enough to leave the arena?"

At their chorus of "yes-s-s," she grinned. "Then bring your lunches on Tuesday—in saddlebags if you have them. You'll need signed permission slips, and I recommend you pack your sandwiches and chips and such in plastic containers so they don't get squished. My friend Amy will be coming along. Any questions?"

All three girls wore matching grins, the kind that wrapped nearly around their heads.

"Now, take care of your horses. I see at least one mother hanging over the fence. Krissie, aren't you in a hurry today?"

"Hey, kitty-cat." DJ heard the nasty voice after she'd just waved her last student off.

"James, I'm gonna . . ." She spun around but couldn't see him anywhere.

"Meow, meow, meow." Now he sounded just like a cat food commercial.

She looked down the aisle again in time to see him duck into Diablo's stall. Why did he always pick on her? Or did he treat everyone this way? She thought about that, all the while letting his taunting set her on a slow burn.

"Kitty-cat, kitty-cat, where are you hiding at?" Now he'd rhymed it.

DJ started down the aisle, fists clenched at her side.

"Hey, DJ, I need some help over here," Amy called from the other end of the barn.

DJ turned and stomped back the way she'd come. She'd have to take care of James later.

"Don't let him bug you," Amy said after one look at DJ's face. "He's not worth getting all mad over."

"He doesn't call *you* names." Without being told to, DJ held the horse while Amy picked its hooves. Since this one had a habit of reaching back to nip once in a while, they took extra precautions.

"As your Gran says, 'sticks and stones . . .' "

"I know what she says, but words *do* hurt. I can't help my green eyes. Nobody else has cat's eyes. He's right."

"So that makes you special."

"Ames, sometimes you sound just like Gran." The two giggled together.

"So, what are you doing for your birthday?" The two were ready to head home.

"I thought maybe you could come over and we'd go

out for pizza and then a movie. Maybe my mom and Gran will go, too."

"You don't want a party?"

DJ shook her head. "Not this year. I think we're going to get enough of birthday parties as it is."

"Hey, Mom and Dad might hire us for Danny's party on August tenth." Amy swung her leg over the seat of her bike. "Great, huh?"

DJ nodded. "Flier is almost done. You want to come eat at my house so we can work on it?"

"I'll ask." The two pedaled hard up and down Reliez Valley Road, coasting down the last hill to their houses.

Sure hope Gran doesn't ask me about James, DJ thought when she braked into her garage. She put her bike away and closed the garage door. She'd been extra careful lately. This was *not* a good time to get her mother mad. But then when was? The thought made her smile. Her mother was due back from another trip tonight. They'd talk about her birthday then.

What if her mother gave her a horse for her fourteenth? Wouldn't that be unbelievable? The thought stopped her from getting a drink at the sink. She closed her eyes, imagining what having her own horse would be like. But when she opened them, reality took hold. The day Lindy Randall bought her daughter a horse would be the day the sky fell.

That evening the girls took their flier to the copy shop and ran off five hundred copies.

"Guess we're in business, partner." Amy stuck out her hand.

"Yup." They shook and grinned at each other. This one would be a winner.

DJ fell asleep that night with twenty dollar bills flitting through her mind.

Her birthday dawned with gray skies but brightened considerably when James' nanny called to say he wouldn't be at the Academy that day. DJ rushed through her work, cleaning stalls at top speed and grooming horses like a robot set on super fast.

"DJ, can you come here a minute?" Bridget called as DJ finished snapping her last horses on the hot walker.

"Sure." DJ trotted across the dusty parking lot and into the office.

"Surprise!" All the kids who worked at the Academy yelled in unison. A chocolate frosted cake with the words *Happy Birthday, DJ* took up half the desk.

Bridget finished lighting the candles. "All right, everyone. Let us sing! 'Happy birthday to you!'" The song filled the room and traveled down the aisle.

DJ looked from face to face, sure that her grin mirrored those of her friends. Amy stood right beside the cake, singing the loudest.

"Okay, make a wish and blow out the candles."

DJ crossed the room and bent over. Panic squeezed her throat shut. She couldn't blow.

7

FOR A HORRIBLE MOMENT, ALL DJ COULD SEE was flickering fire. Her heart pounded louder than any drum. She couldn't tear her gaze away from the burning candles in front of her.

DJ licked her lips. They were so dry.

One hand curled around the scarred palm of the other to protect it. She remembered the sensation of the fire searing her hand, remembered thinking she would never escape it. She was lost again in the terror of that day.

"DJ! DJ!"

DJ heard a voice. Someone was shaking her. *Bridget!*

"The fire." Her words croaked past a throat burning from smoke. DJ shook her head. It was a birthday party. Just a cake. She was to blow out the candles. She looked down. Only tiny spirals of smoke rose from the green candles.

Happy Birthday, DJ. The letters were green, too. A brown horse jumped a fence below the words.

DJ forced her eyes to blink. To look at her friends. Amy had tears running down her face. Bridget's face was mercifully expressionless. The others were as embarrassed to look at her as she was at them.

"I . . . I'm sorry, DJ, I forgot. I'm so sorry."

DJ could hear Amy's wail, but it seemed far off. As if it were coming from the end of a long tunnel.

Only Bridget's arm around her shaking shoulders kept DJ in place. "No problem. We wanted to surprise you. I guess we did just that." Bridget squeezed again. "Hilary, you cut the cake. Daniel, you serve the ice cream." While the others bustled around, looking relieved at having something to do, Bridget leaned closer. "Are you all right now?"

DJ nodded. "It's never been that bad before."

"You've never had so many candles." Amy clung to DJ's left arm. "I'm sorry, DJ. I should have thought."

"Has it always been like this?" Bridget spoke for DJ's ears alone.

"When I was real little, I was somehow caught in a fire and burned." She held up her hand and showed the scar in the palm. "I've been afraid of fire ever since." DJ looked up. "Dumb, isn't it?"

"No, not dumb." Bridget relaxed her arm. "Here, take my chair, the place of honor. You think you can eat your cake and ice cream now?"

DJ nodded. "Sure." But she felt like crawling under the chair rather than sitting in it. Under the chair, then under the desk, and out the door. At least James wasn't there.

"I just wanted to celebrate your birthday," Amy said later, after the others had left and they'd cleaned up the trash. The expression on her face would have made a Basset hound look happy.

"Thanks, Ames. It isn't your fault I'm such a geek about fires. Even little ones like birthday candles." DJ studied the half-burned green stems of wax. "How could I have freaked like that?"

"Do you have nightmares about the accident?" Bridget asked, elbows on her desk.

"I used to. But I haven't for a long time." DJ straightened a stack of papers on the corner. While her heart rate had returned to normal, the tips of her fingers still trembled.

"Thank you both for surprising me like this. And for the cake and everything. I'm glad I have friends like you."

"Now we're getting mushy." Amy grinned and punched DJ's shoulder. "Let's hit the bikes. We're supposed to hand out fliers this afternoon, remember?"

DJ groaned. "How could I forget?"

"You two be careful now, you hear?" Bridget called after them as they left the building.

Putting a flier on every door in the neighborhood sounded easy but took plenty of time. Amy's two brothers helped, but even so, by the time five o'clock rolled around, they hadn't finished.

DJ eyed the stack she still carried. The sweat from her arm had wrinkled the bottom one. She tossed it in the trash and collapsed on the front steps of her house, along with Amy and her older brother John. Twelve-year-old Dan hadn't returned yet.

"How'd you guys do?"

Identical groans answered her.

"One old man yelled at me," Amy said without opening her eyes. "He accused me of not being able to read."

"Read what?" John asked.

"His *no solicitors* sign."

"Did you tell him you're in the honors program at

school?" John propped himself up on his elbows.

"No, the sign was hidden by a bush. How was I supposed to see it?"

"So, did you give him a flier?" John winked at DJ.

"Yeah, right." She glared up at him on the step above her. "Besides, he was too old to have little kids."

"Maybe he has grandchildren." John tweaked her braid.

"Nah, he's too mean."

"Hey, guys. I have a number for a lady who wants you to call her." Dan pedaled up the street and let his bike drop on the grass.

"DJ, telephone," Gran announced through the screen door.

Within the hour, they had three bookings. DJ and Amy rushed to the door as soon as they heard Lindy's car. "Mom, guess what?"

"You're ready to go for pizza. Please, I need some time off first." Lindy shut off the engine and started to open the door.

"No—well, yes—but even better. We have three parties to give! And we just gave out the fliers today."

"And we're not even finished." Amy waved the paper they'd written all the information on.

"We had to turn a Saturday party down because of our horse show, so the woman said they'd have the party Sunday after church instead. Cool, huh?"

"Cool is right. How about pouring me some cool iced tea. My air conditioner is on the blink." She brushed her hair off her forehead.

An hour later, Lindy, Gran, and the two girls climbed into Gran's minivan and headed for the Pizza House.

When Lindy asked how the day had been, DJ sank

back into her chair. Amy gave her a poke in the ribs.

"Oh, they gave me a birthday cake at the Academy. I freaked at the candles. No big deal." DJ threw in a shruggy laugh and looked up at the faces of her mother and Gran. "Really, it was nothing."

Gran looked at Amy.

Amy looked from DJ to Gran and then to Lindy. "It *was* a big deal. She scared us all half to bits. She freaked. It was as if she weren't even there." She grimaced at DJ and shook her head. "I have to be honest." She looked back at Gran. "She froze."

"Thanks a lot, buddy." The tone said the name meant anything but.

"I thought you'd outgrown your fear of fire." Lindy spoke softly, her comment a question.

"I did too. So I guess I haven't."

The restaurant loudspeaker crackled. "Number 43."

"That's us." DJ leaped to her feet, nearly toppling her bench at the rush.

When the cupcake came and the waiters and waitresses gathered around to help sing, there was no candle burning bright. DJ didn't know whether to be glad or sad. She caught a wink from Gran. She knew they'd be talking about this later.

"Open that one first." Lindy pointed to a big square box.

DJ tossed Amy the ribbon and tore off the paper. Nested in a crinkle of tissue paper lay a red cowboy hat with white lacing around the edge. "Thanks, Mom." DJ handed it to Amy. "We're in business now."

"Now this one." Lindy handed her daughter a flat box that looked as though it held clothes.

"Wow!" DJ held up a starched white shirt. "And jodhpurs." She caressed the tan twill fabric. "They're perfect."

"I hope they fit. Your others were looking pretty shabby."

"Thanks, Mom."

"Well, I figured when you start jumping, new duds would help." She handed DJ another box. "This one's from both Gran and me together." A black hunt coat with a store-bought label lay folded in front of her.

DJ looked up at both her mother and Gran. "You guys didn't have to do this. It must have cost a bundle." *And with Diablo gone, I won't even get to show.* When she looked at Amy, she could read the same thought on her face. "Thanks, Mom, Gran. Now, you don't have to spend your time sewing me a new one."

"A labor of love, my dear. But now that you're so grown up, you deserve a professionally tailored coat."

Amy handed DJ a package wrapped in paper covered with jumping horses. "Here, I know you needed these."

The box contained a new set of charcoal pencils and two thick pads of drawing paper.

"You're right. Thanks, now I don't have to raid my horse fund." DJ closed all the boxes and piled them at the end of the table. "What a super, fantastic, wonderful birthday."

"If we're going to see a movie, we better hustle." Lindy picked up the check. "Come on."

DJ tucked all the boxes under her arm. The next thing she'd need would be boots. Hers were beginning to pinch in the toe. If only she'd quit growing!

She tuned back into the conversation between her mother and Gran.

"But I don't really care to meet anyone," Gran was saying.

"Now, Mother, Joe Crowder is one of the nicest men I've ever met. I think the two of you will get along famously." Lindy held the door open for all of them. "Besides, I invited him over for dinner a week from Sunday. And I know you'll like him, too, Darla Jean. He's head of the horse patrol in San Francisco."

"He's a policeman?" DJ spun around to stare at her mother.

"And a good one. His wife died two years ago. I've known him for a long time, and I can tell he's lonely."

"You invited a policeman to our house? The whole neighborhood will think we're being arrested!" DJ couldn't resist the smart remark.

"He won't come in a squad car, silly." Lindy slid into the front seat of the minivan. "Besides, how would I meet any men outside a police force?"

For some reason, DJ had a bad feeling in her stomach.

8

"OKAY, RIDERS UP." DJ CHECKED HER students one more time.

"Oh, wait, I forgot my drink." Angie withdrew her foot from the stirrup. "I'll be right back."

While she was gone, DJ and Amy checked everyone's cinches for the third time. "All the rest of you sure you have everything?" At their chorus of yes's, DJ signaled Amy to mount while she led Megs and Angie's horse to the front of the barn. She crossed to the gate of the trail to Briones State Park and opened it, signaling them through. While she waited, she checked her saddlebags again to make sure she had the beesting kit. Angie had asthma and was violently allergic to beestings.

Angie rushed up as the last horse trailed through the gate. "Thanks, DJ. My mom says to give you an extra thanks from her. She's looking forward to a day off."

"You're welcome. Up you go now." After leading Megs through, DJ closed the gate, making sure the latch fell into place. One time the gate had accidentally been left open, and a horse had run away.

With DJ in front and Amy bringing up the rear, the group headed single file up the hill. Oak trees dotted the

71

steep hillsides where the trail led along the flank of another rounded hump, then down to the staging area and parking lot for the Reliez Valley entrance to Briones Park. Beef cow and calf pairs roamed the pastureland, along with young steers. One calf with a white face and black body ran off, tail in the air at the sight of the trail horses. Several others followed.

"Watch your horses." DJ kept a secure hand on her reins. "They could spook easily."

Once on the shady trail that followed the creek up into the park, the kids could ride side by side. A stellar jay scolded them from one of the branches, flitting along as if trying to convince them to go back. The curious calves plodded behind, making the girls giggle.

"We're supposed to *herd* cattle rather than lead them," Krissie called. "DJ, you ever tried cutting cows from a herd?"

"No way. Besides, Ames here rides Western, not me."

Once they reached the high meadow, the girls voted to ride up to the Briones Crest Trail. From there they could see the Carquinez Straits and up the Sacramento River to the north. The oil refineries below looked like a toy Erector set with their towers and round storage tanks.

"What are those boxes on the fence?" Krissie asked.

"Bluebird nests. Since so many of their natural nesting spots are gone, people have put these up to encourage them to stick around."

"How do you know so much?"

DJ and Amy swapped grins. "When we rode up here with Hilary, we asked the same question and she gave us the answer. Maybe someday you'll be doing the same for other kids."

"Can we peek in one?"

"If a mother is nesting, you might frighten her off the nest. Would you like that?"

All the girls shook their heads.

"Oh, look!" Sam pointed into the air. A hawk dove straight down, then lifted off again with something dangling from its talons.

"He killed something."

"Yuk."

"No fair." The girls voiced their disapproval.

"Probably a ground squirrel or mouse. That's the way of life. You want him to starve to death?"

"It could be he's taking it home to his family." Amy shaded her eyes with her hand. "He is so beautiful."

After lunch the girls flopped back on the ground.

"I want to come up here every week." Krissie rolled over on her stomach, clenching her lead rope in one hand. They'd removed their horses' bridles and snapped lead lines to the halters. "If we lived in olden times, we could hobble our horses and spend the night."

"The older kids get to take a pack trip up in the Sierra Mountains every summer. You have that to look forward to." Amy tucked her gear back in her saddlebag.

"You ever done that?"

"Nope. Not yet, maybe next summer."

DJ shook her head, too. You had to have your own horse for that trip. And she knew Amy had waited because DJ couldn't go. Maybe by next summer she'd have a horse of her own. Not maybe. When.

"I want to go on the overnight."

"Well, think positive, and you'll make it." DJ wasn't sure if she was talking to herself or to her students.

She breathed a sigh of relief when they rode back

into the academy parking lot. They'd had a great time—not a single bee in sight.

"How did it go?" Bridget asked when DJ and Amy stopped in at her office.

"Fine."

"Great."

"Good, because the girls were bubbling over. Oh, DJ, your grandmother called. Said for you to hurry right home."

"Is she all right?" DJ started for the door.

"She's fine. She was laughing, said the phone has not stopped ringing. I think you two are going to be mighty busy young women. Just make sure you keep up with your chores around here."

"We will." DJ pushed Amy out the door ahead of her. Visions of a horse of her own jumped through her mind.

Saturday morning DJ and Amy arrived at the Academy before six to help load horses in the trailers to take them to the show. The first event would be at nine.

"Your mom and dad coming later?" DJ asked.

"Uh-huh. The boys too. I have four events today." Amy yawned. "Dad's coming to help trailer Josh. Says he's sure glad we don't own a truck and trailer."

At least you have a horse, DJ wanted to say but didn't. Sometimes the little green monster of jealousy got her by the throat.

If only Diablo were here! How can I stand by and watch all the others out in the ring? She'd gone to sleep with that question and woke without an answer.

"Just keep real busy today," Gran had whispered in

her ear just before DJ went out the door. "I'll be praying for you."

"God, please help me." DJ added a prayer of her own. *Oh, Diablo, I miss you so!*

By the time the sixteen horses were loaded, DJ had sweat pouring down her face and back. Hilary, the oldest and most experienced of the working students and a skilled rider in dressage, had to drive home to retrieve the duffel bag she'd forgotten. One family overslept. Bridget wore that stern look that said she'd get everyone there on time even if it killed her—and them.

After one longing look at Diablo's stall, DJ hadn't had time to give him another thought. "How come James isn't here to load his own horse?" she muttered as she passed Amy, who was heading back into the barn for another animal.

"Got me." Amy brushed her bangs off her forehead. "Today's gonna be a scorcher."

DJ clucked to Gray Bar, James' Arabian filly. "Easy, girl. You just keep calm and we'll all have a better day." They trotted across the parking lot, Gray Bar dancing along with DJ. But the filly sat back on her haunches as soon as she touched her front feet to the ramp.

"We would have one troublemaker." Hilary's father, better known to the academy kids as Dad, stood beside the trailer. He'd been assisting Hilary since she was seven, so knew a lot about loading horses.

"Come on, girl." DJ tugged on the lead rope. The filly snorted, her eyes rolling white.

"Walk her around in a circle and bring her up again," Dad said in a soft but commanding voice.

DJ did as he instructed, but again Gray Bar balked. When DJ tugged the rope, the filly flung her head in the air and backed up fast. The sliding rope burned through her palm. Repeating the sequence, she followed the horse, this time keeping a tight grip on the lead.

"Let's leave her 'til last. Why don't you just walk her around and let her calm down."

"Would it be better to wait for her owner?" asked one of the newer fathers. Dad shook his head. "DJ can handle her better than James."

DJ felt a warm glow tiptoe into her chest. Leave it to Dad to always make her feel good. But when she led Gray Bar around the truck, there sat James on the bumper. The look he gave her doused the warm feeling like water drenching a fire.

When DJ offered him the lead rope, James shook his head. "You're so good, you do it."

DJ shrugged and kept walking. When they brought Gray Bar back around a few minutes later, she walked right up the ramp as if there'd been no fiasco. But DJ knew there'd been a problem. Her hand still stung.

DJ kept so busy helping the younger kids, she hardly had time to miss not being in the arena. Lost hair ribbons, making sure the entry numbers were pinned on the right rider, catching a loose horse—it was all part of a show.

Amy won three blues, her best ever.

"Congratulations, Ames. You looked great out there."

"All the hard work with Josh here is paying off." Amy chugged a can of soda. "These chaps are killing me. One more class and I can change to shorts."

"DJ, I can't find my saddle pad," a worried-looking student interrupted their conversation.

DJ turned to find it and caught a glimpse of James in the ring. His horse was refusing the gate in the trail-riding event. Just as she'd done at the loading, Gray Bar backed up fast—so fast she threw James up onto her neck. DJ felt her breath catch in her throat. She didn't wish anyone, even James, a fall in the ring. How embarrassing!

A few minutes later he stormed past her. "If you hadn't gotten her so excited this morning, I might be doing better out there."

The words and their tone caught DJ smack in the middle. "James Corrigan, I . . ."

He gave her a rude gesture and slammed the door on his parents' motorhome.

"I wish you'd fallen!" DJ felt like yanking open the door and pounding him into the carpet.

By the end of the day, the riders from the Academy had garnered a good fifty percent of the ribbons, many of them blue or red. Bridget congratulated everyone while they loaded horses and weary kids.

"Any of you who want to come up to the house for a pool party afterward are welcome. Mr. Yamamoto and Mr. Benson have volunteered to bring pizza."

A cheer went up. DJ was too tired to care.

Maybe having a stable of her own one day wasn't such a hot idea after all.

"Tomorrow we have our first pony party," DJ groaned later as she and Amy lay beside the pool. Most of the other kids were still in the water.

"I know. But there are only supposed to be five kids at this one. That should be easy."

"Oh, it should be, all right." DJ shook her head. "But after today, who knows what could happen!"

9

"NO, JAMIE, DON'T FEED THAT TO THE PONY."

DJ spun around at the sound of Amy's voice. The five kids at the pony party now seemed like a squadron. With one hand DJ snatched the pink flower from the little boy's hand, and with the other she set him back five feet. Then she returned to putting the cowboy hat back on the little girl seated on Bandit.

"No, don't want no hat!" The child jerked the Western hat off and threw it on the ground.

Bandit sidestepped, the better to see the flying object. DJ followed, one hand on the pommel and the other holding the little girl in place. Amy hung on to the reins, trying to calm the pony, her camera on a strap around her neck.

"Who ever came up with this harebrained idea?" DJ muttered through the smile she kept in place for the child's benefit. "Okay, no hat. Now hang on to the saddle horn—this thing"—she placed the girl's hand on the horn—"and I'll lead you around. Then smile for Amy and you'll get a picture to take home."

The little girl stuck out her lower lip.

DJ led her around the drive. Bandit stopped at the

halfway point to make manure. *Oops, should have brought a shovel*. DJ looked up at Amy, who shrugged her shoulders.

"I'll take care of it in a minute." Amy snapped the photo. The little girl smiled and waved. Afterward.

By the last rider, it seemed as though they'd taken fifteen terrors around the circle. At least no one had fallen off or slipped. Amy went up to the door to ask for a shovel.

"Time for cake and ice cream," the hostess mother called when she answered Amy's knock at the front door. Three children ran right through the pile of manure and into the house.

"Icky," whined the grumpy rider.

"Oh no, my white carpet!" The mother glared at Amy. "I hope this washes out. We just had the carpet installed last week."

"It will." Amy mentioned a brand of cleaner her mother used. "I need a shovel, please."

"You certainly do. And I hope you're not planning on putting that mess in *my* garbage can."

"I could put it on your flower beds, it'll help—"

"I should say not. I'll bring the shovel. And the carpet cleaner."

Amy turned back to DJ and raised her hands.

By the time Amy had cleaned the carpet and DJ the drive, the kids had eaten their treats, opened presents, and were ready to ride again.

"No, dears, the pony has to go home now." The woman smiled brightly as she handed DJ an envelope with their fee in it in exchange for the stack of photos. "Thank you for such a perfect party. I'll be sure to recommend you to all my friends."

DJ and Amy looked at each other, shrugged, and headed for home.

"Go figure." Amy shook her head. "The way she talked at first I didn't think she'd even pay us."

"It must have been her first time giving a birthday party. She was pretty uptight."

"Who wouldn't be with new white carpet? My mom says she's not getting new furniture and carpet 'til all us kids are grown and gone." Bandit snorted as if in agreement.

"What a good boy you were." DJ stopped to rub the pony's neck. "But you shouldn't take bites out of the flower bed."

"How'd it go?" Hilary asked when they hung Bandit's bridle on his peg in the tack room. She wiped the sweat off her wide brow with the back of her brown hand and pushed back tightly curled black hair that refused to obey a ponytail clip.

"Oh, it went." By the time they finished telling their tale, Hilary had collapsed on the tack box, tears running down her face.

"You poor kids, talk about a party! Now that all the bad stuff has happened, the next one'll be a cinch." She rocked back with her hands around one knee. "You *are* going to keep going, aren't you?"

"We have to. We signed people up." Amy counted on her fingers. "We have eight more parties to go."

"And that's if no one else calls." DJ squeezed her eyes shut. "Next time I have a good idea, someone shoot me, okay?"

"Don't tempt me." Amy grabbed DJ's hand and pulled her to her feet. "I gotta get home. And remember, you've got company coming for dinner."

DJ groaned louder but let herself be led from the building. "Well, at least the next party will be profit."

"Unless we buy a pooper scooper. You know, like the ones they use at parades."

"I think the Academy has one. I'll ask Bridget if we can borrow it." DJ mounted her ten speed. "At least I'll be able to put money in my horse fund after Tuesday."

When DJ got home, the table was set in the dining room with a jade green cloth and matching print napkins—in napkin rings no less. Gran's good china and sterling silver were set for four. Green candles flanked a low arrangement of peach roses.

"Wow, does this look cool or what? What's the name of that man who's coming?"

"Joe Crowder, Captain Joe Crowder." Lindy turned from arranging salad on separate plates.

"Right. He must be something pretty special. It's not Christmas or Easter, is it?"

"You just hustle up and shower. And no jeans. In fact, a dress would be nice."

"That'll be the day." DJ pulled a can of soda from the fridge.

"I don't need that kind of attitude right now." Mom swiped a hair off her forehead with the back of her hand.

"I mean, I don't have a dress to wear." Surely her mother had lost her mind.

"A skirt then."

DJ groaned. "Skirts are gross." After popping the can top, she took a long drink. "Where's Gran?" Her mother hadn't done all the cooking—had she? That would be bad.

"She's changing." Lindy wrapped the salad plates in plastic wrap and set them in the fridge.

"What are we having?" Her mother's skill ran to hamburgers or spaghetti. If it didn't come in a box, she couldn't make it.

"Are you going to get ready or not?"

DJ wanted to say "not" but thought the better of it. Her mother didn't look as if she were in the mood for any teasing. "I'm going, I'm going." *She could at least have asked about our pony party*, DJ thought as she climbed the stairs. *Leave it to my mother not to ask. She's more worried about a dinner party for a man she hardly knows than about her own daughter.* If she gave it some effort, DJ knew she could turn this evening into a full-blown pity party. "Wow, Gran, you look amazing."

Gran spun away from studying her reflection in the full-length mirror at the end of the hall. "I hope so. Your mother spent a fortune on this new outfit for me. I feel as if I'm on the auction block or something." She turned so the skirt swirled about her calves.

"That looks like something you might have painted." DJ fingered the gauze fabric. "All swirly and all shades of blue. Leave it to Mom to find the perfect thing."

Gran turned and placed her hands along DJ's cheeks. "Thanks, darlin'. How did the birthday party go?" Gran laughed in all the right places as DJ retold the story. "Well, I never. And to think she made you girls clean the carpet!"

"Amy did that." DJ patted her jeans pocket. "But at least all our bills are paid. Now we can make some money."

Gran took one more glance over her shoulder toward the mirror. "Well, here goes nothin'." She started toward the stairs. "Oh, my stars, where's my mind today! DJ, there was another call for you. A lady wondered if you could come tomorrow. Her clown called with the flu. I put the number on your dresser."

"Thanks, I'll call her now." DJ dialed, dollar signs dancing in her head.

She could hear a man's voice in the living room by the time she descended the stairs. Her skirt had been too tight, so she had improvised with a pair of dress pants and a striped blouse. No T-shirt and jeans. She paused at the bottom stair. At least the guy knew how to laugh.

Hearing a man's laugh in their house was sure strange. The pastor from their church had been their most recent male visitor, and that had been ages ago. His laugh hadn't had the deep, happy sound of the man's in the living room.

"Hi, darlin'," Gran said when DJ walked into the room. She beckoned DJ to her side. "This is my granddaughter, Darla Jean. She's a real promising artist, but her first love is horses."

DJ barely kept herself from wincing. *Darla Jean.* Only her Gran, and sometimes her mother, got away with calling her that. She didn't want this stranger calling her that. "Darlin', this is Joe Crowder."

"Well, Darla Jean, I certainly am glad to meet you." The voice fit the man. He took up half the living room, or at least seemed to. Shoulders straight and square like a military man's, a crew cut gone silver, and cerulean blue eyes.

"I'm glad to meet you, too. Mom said you like horses."

"You'll have to meet my best friend sometime. His name is Major. I've ridden him in the San Francisco Mounted Patrol for the last ten years."

"What's he like?"

"Thoroughbred-Morgan cross. Sixteen-three. He has to be big to carry me. White stripe down his face, two white socks. He's a blood bay, the prettiest red you ever saw when the sun glints off his rump. Even has a scar on his right shoulder where he took a bullet meant for me."

"Really?"

"You ever watched the mounted patrol in action?"

DJ shook her head.

"Then I'll have to take you and Melanie to watch one of our drills."

DJ almost looked around the room for the Melanie he'd referred to. "You mean Gran?"

"Dinner's served." Lindy stopped in the doorway.

DJ rolled her eyes so only Gran could see. The look clearly said what she thought of the formality. But when Joe Crowder tucked Gran's arm in one of his and angled out his other elbow for DJ to do the same, she went along with it. Who was this guy anyway?

She was wondering even more by the end of the meal. He'd had them all laughing at his tales of life in the mounted patrol. And the stories about his family. He had three kids, two sons and a daughter. The daughter had two children, including a girl who was only a year older than DJ.

"Robert, my oldest, is a widower like me. He has five-year-old twin boys."

"That must have been really hard." Gran reached across the space and laid her hand on his.

"It was. To lose two women in our family in one year." He sighed. "I can't wait for you to meet them. I know they'll like you . . ." He cut off the sentence, but his eyes said the rest.

DJ dropped her fork. She'd read about talking with your eyes before, but now she was seeing it in action. The way those two were looking at each other usually meant a love scene coming up in the movies.

She glanced at her mother. Lindy wore a sappy look that said she was happy with the whole thing.

"Can I be excused? I . . . I'll clear the table." *Anything to get out of here.*

"I'll help you." Mom pushed her chair back, too.

The other two in the room didn't even seem to notice.

A cold hand slipped over DJ's heart and squeezed.

10

"THAT WAS DISGUSTING!"

"I don't know, I think they're kind of cute." Lindy opened the dishwasher door.

"Cute!" DJ spun around, catching a plate before it slid off the counter.

"Shhh, keep your voice down or they'll hear you."

"Cute. Gran and a man she just met are making goo-goo eyes at each other and *my* mother thinks it's cute."

"Careful, you said you'd wash the dishes, not break them." Mom took over the sink detail. "You finish clearing the table."

"I can't go in there again." DJ clamped her hands on her hips.

"Darla Jean Randall, for pete's sake, grow up!" Lindy's voice changed from teasing to angry. "We've had a very nice time tonight, and I don't want to see you ruining it. Your grandmother is entitled to a little love in her life."

"She had Grandpa."

"And he died ten years ago. She has spent the last ten years taking care of you and me."

"She has her art, you know. And her garden and

87

books and church and . . ." DJ let the words trail off.

"And you. If I'd been a better mother, she wouldn't have had to spend her life raising her granddaughter."

"You said it, I didn't." The words popped out before DJ could trap her tongue. She headed for the dining room. Sometimes retreating made more sense than fighting.

There was no one there. DJ drifted over to the windows that overlooked the backyard. Gran was showing Joe her roses. The two of them didn't have to stand so close together.

"Stupid birds, you don't have to sing so loud, do you?" DJ covered her head with her pillow early the next morning. But when she closed her eyes again, all she could see was Gran smiling up at that old policeman as though he were the last man on earth. She flung back the covers and stomped down the hall to the bathroom. Maybe things would go better over at the Academy.

"Mornin', darlin', you're up early." Gran sat in her chair in front of the bay window, Bible in her lap and her hair in the normal disarray.

Maybe I'm blowing this all out of proportion. The thought zipped through DJ's mind like the humming-birds at their feeders. *Gran was just being polite. Southern women are supposed to be polite and gracious. She's trying to show me how to be the same way.* After popping a slice of wheat bread in the toaster, DJ pulled the pitcher of orange juice out of the fridge and poured herself a glass. She spread peanut butter on the toast and took her juice and toast into the other room where she sat at Gran's feet.

"So, what's on your schedule for today?" Gran laid a hand on DJ's head.

"The usual. Then we have that pony party this afternoon. You want some help in the garden when I get home?"

"Thank you, dear, but no thanks. Joe and I are going to a concert this evening."

DJ jerked out from under the loving hand and twisted around to look up at her grandmother. *What a sappy look!* "You mean you're going out with him—like on a date?" Her voice squeaked on the final word.

"I guess you could call it that." Gran smiled. "He's really a nice man, don't you think?"

DJ gave a decidedly unladylike snort. So much for her grandmother's training. "If you like old men, I guess."

"Darla Jean, why I'm surprised at you." Gran leaned forward and lifted DJ's chin with gentle fingers. "Look at me, child. He's only ten years older than I am."

"But . . . but you're not old. Why, you're not even fifty yet." DJ tried to look at her grandmother as if she were seeing her for the first time. All she could see was the love shining in her grandmother's eyes. "You . . . you're my gran. You're beautiful."

"Why, thank you, but fifty really isn't far off." Gran put her cheek next to DJ's. "I love you more than words can ever say." She straightened up. "If I only had time to sew a new dress."

DJ pushed to her feet. "The one you wore yesterday sure made him look twice—if that's what you want." She left the room, her thudding heels leaving no doubt as to her opinion.

"You're acting like a brat," she scolded herself as she pumped up the hill. "Gran looks happy as a kid with a Popsicle, and you want to take it away from her." The climb made her puff. *You can't get along with your mother, and now you're grumbling at Gran. Grow up!*

After DJ had finished her beginners' class, she entered the office to check the duties board. Bridget called her in for a conference, her expression serious.

"DJ, James said that you took the missing bridle and saddle."

"He's crazy! Why would I do that?"

"That's what I asked him. He said you were going to sell it so you would have more money to put in your horse fund."

"And you believed him?" DJ clenched her hands. *Why would Bridget believe James over her?*

"I did not say that. I just have to follow up on every lead. We have never had a problem with things being stolen before." Bridget leaned forward, her elbows on her desk. "So if you tell me you did not take it, then I will know for sure you did not."

"I didn't take that tack or anything else." DJ forced the words through gritted teeth. *That ... that lying, cheating, lazy, good for nothing creep!* "Is there anything else?" All she could think of was getting out of there, finding James and—what could she do to him that was bad enough?

"DJ, do not take this personally."

But DJ was already out the door.

"What's the matter, DJ?" Hilary tried to grab DJ's arm and missed.

"Where's James?"

"He just left. Said he had a headache." She rolled her eyes. "You know James."

"That lazy little creep, I'm gonna kill him."

Hilary fell into step beside her. "What'd he do now?"

"Told Bridget I stole a new saddle and bridle."

Hilary let out a bark of laughter. "He what? DJ, surely Bridget doesn't believe him. Come on, be real!"

"I think he hates me."

"So what? James hates everybody. Anyway, most everybody—around here at least—returns the favor." Hilary plunked down on a bale of straw. "Here." She patted the bale beside her. "You've just got to develop a thick skin. James is jealous because he's been taking lessons longer and you ride better than he does."

"But he has his own horse. He could ride all the time if he wanted, practice until he gets everything perfect."

"DJ, that's the way *you* do things because you have a goal. Like me with dressage."

"You're good." DJ clasped her hands between her knees.

"I've worked hard to get there. And I'll keep on working hard. Just like you do. So don't let this get to you. James isn't worth it."

DJ nodded. As usual, Hilary made sense. "Thanks. It just seems to me that if you've got your own horse and you can ride whenever you want . . ."

"That everything should be all right."

DJ nodded. "Wrong, huh?" She could feel her grin coming back.

"Wrong is right." Hilary slapped DJ on the knee. "So let's get back to work." She got to her feet. "Okay, now?"

"Okay." But inside, DJ thought only two things. How

would she get even with James? And who had taken the tack? A new flat saddle and a good bridle—why, that kind of equipment was worth hundreds of dollars.

DJ and Amy trotted Bandit down the shoulder of Reliez Valley Road. If they didn't hurry, they'd be late. The pooper scooper they had borrowed and tied to the saddle clapped against the pony's side with each quick stride.

"We need a cart for him to pull all of our stuff in." DJ puffed between words.

"Not a bad idea." Amy jogged along, the lead strap in her hands. "Is Bandit used to the harness?"

"Got me! If he was, we could ride, too." Down a hill and around the corner. "If he hasn't been broken to the cart, he will be soon."

"Hey, Mom, the pony's here." A little boy met them in the drive. His shriek made Bandit lay back his ears.

"Here we go again," DJ whispered to Amy.

"No, this party's going to go great. I've been praying about it."

DJ felt a surge of guilt. Why hadn't she thought of that?

"You should have prayed harder," DJ grumbled when a little boy refused to get off the pony. Instead, he let out a scream that brought the mothers running to see who was attacking their kids.

"Now, Robert, honey," the mother said soothingly. "You have to give the other children a turn."

"N-o-o-o! I want another ride." Robert clung to the saddle horn like a flea to a dog.

The mother smiled apologetically. "Maybe you could take him around one more time. I'm sure he'll get off then. Won't you, dear?"

DJ and Amy swapped raised-eyebrow glances. They knew they were thinking the same thing. If Amy's brothers had tried something like that, her mother wouldn't have let them get away with it.

The little girl who was next in line started to cry. The other mothers glared at Robert's mom. DJ led Bandit once more around the circle.

"If you don't get off when you get back, I'm gonna let this pony gallop down the street with you on his back, and you'll go splat on the pavement." She kept her tone low, muttering just loud enough so she knew Robert heard. When she looked at him, his eyes were wide. "I will, too."

Robert jumped right off and ran to his mother, where he clutched at the back of her pants.

The rest of the party went as planned. All the kids rode and smiled for their pictures. The hostess even brought DJ and Amy glasses of icy lemonade.

"Thanks. We needed that." DJ drank half of hers without stopping.

"Would you be interested in bringing the pony to the park one day and just letting kids ride like this? It wouldn't be for a party." The mother looked from DJ to Amy.

The two girls looked at each other and shrugged. "I guess so." Amy spoke first.

"What would you charge for an hour? No pictures."

DJ named a figure and Amy agreed.

"Good, I'll get back to you." The woman handed them an envelope and started to leave. "Oh, I'm sorry about the problem with Robert. He's a bit spoiled."

"He's a *bit* spoiled!" The two girls hooted when they were a block or two away. They took the money out of the envelope and split it. With the bills already paid, this could become a very successful project.

"That much more for my horse fund." DJ stuck the bills in her pocket. "Wish it were twice this much."

"Or ten times." Amy stopped trotting to retie the pooper scooper before it fell off. "You want to talk to Bridget about harness training Bandit, or should I?"

"Let's do it together. There's that harness buried in the tack room. That should fit him fine. I haven't seen any carts around there though, have you?"

Amy shook her head. "Bridget will know of one."

But Bridget was busy with a class when they got back to the Academy, so as soon as they'd given Bandit a good grooming, they jumped on their bikes to head for home.

"Gran? Gran?" DJ wandered through the house, calling. When there was no answer, she headed for the backyard. Gran's minivan was in the drive, so she had to be around here somewhere.

"I'm out here."

DJ followed the voice to the backyard. She could see Gran's pink rear when she knelt to pull weeds from the flower bed. "I'm home."

"Good." Gran straightened up and wiped the back of her gloved hand across her forehead. "Would you like to bring us out some lemonade?"

"I told you I'd help you weed tonight."

Gran rocked back on her heels. "I know. I was just too restless to paint anymore today."

DJ gave her a look that questioned whether they'd better head for the hospital emergency room, but she turned and headed back for the kitchen without commenting. That in itself was a miracle, she reminded herself while pouring their drinks. How come it was easier to keep the lid on her mouth with Gran than her mother? Maybe Gran had changed her mind and was staying home from the concert.

"So, how was the party?" Gran sat cross-legged on the grass and reached up for her drink. Her wide floppy straw hat caught in the breeze and flipped back behind her.

DJ sank down beside her, not answering until she'd poured a few glugs down her thirsty throat. As she relayed the story of her day, she sneaked glances at her grandmother. It was clear that she wasn't hearing a word. *Where is she?*

"And so I bopped Amy on the head to make her shut up, and . . ."

"That's nice, dear." Gran sighed.

DJ tried to follow Gran's gaze to see what was so interesting. Grass. Flowers. Pretty, to be sure, but . . .

DJ tried again. "Then I slapped the little kid upside the head . . ."

"Good." Gran handed DJ back the glass. "You want to finish weeding? I think I'll go take a shower and get ready." The older woman rose to her feet and drifted over to the French doors off the deck.

DJ stared after her for a moment before slamming the glass down on the lawn. Jerking weeds out of the ground was probably better than jerking the hairs out of a certain policeman's head. When she stabbed herself on a hidden thistle, she said a word she was glad Gran wasn't around to hear. Maybe getting a horse wasn't her biggest problem after all.

11

"YOU LYING LITTLE—LITTLE ZIT!" AT THE moment DJ couldn't think of anything worse. "I could pound you so far into the dirt, not even your hair would show."

"You and who else, jerk face?" James stood plastered against the stall wall. Six inches shorter than DJ but snarling like a cornered bobcat, he traded insult for insult. "You think you know everything, cat eyes."

DJ clamped her hands to her sides, knowing that if she touched him, she would pound until . . .

"What is going on here? DJ! James! Both of you, out of that stall this instant."

"But she . . ."

"I do not want to hear it. Up to the office! Now!"

DJ could feel the flames burst from inside and turn her skin to fire. Bridget never tolerated fighting on the grounds. And here DJ had been right in the middle of one! With James. She shot him another murderous glare, spun around, and stomped her way to the office. She could hear James behind her trying to make excuses. It wouldn't do any good. Bridget did not accept excuses. If you blew it, you better admit it. Thoughts raged inside her.

What kind of self-discipline lets a creep like James get through? If you can't control your anger over a stupid thing like this, how can you handle the stress of big-time competition? DJ tried to ignore the question, but the guilt that rode her shoulders felt like a pair of Percherons.

She straightened her spine and crossed her arms over her chest when Bridget walked in, trailed by James. DJ glared pitchforks at him, tines first. "I'm sorry I let him get to me like that." She forced the words from between clenched teeth.

Bridget nodded.

DJ stood even straighter and dropped her arms to her sides. Bridget's look said she'd better try again. *Why is Bridget picking on me? After all, James started it.* DJ dug deeper. She could feel the heat on her face, as surely as if she were standing in front of a roaring fire. "I . . . I'm sorry I fought like that. I should have been able to control my temper." She breathed a sigh of relief. The slight softening of Bridget's mouth meant she'd passed.

"James."

James slouched in a chair, arms across his chest, refusing to look at DJ. Or Bridget. He seemed to be studying a dirt spot on his jeans.

"James." The word cracked like a whip.

"Sorry."

Sure, thought DJ. *You really look sorry*. Instantly her mind flashed to herself. Was she sorry? Truly sorry? Or did she just want to get back in Bridget's good graces? The urge to chew on her thumbnail made her hand twitch. But then she'd get a look from Bridget for that.

Instead, she bit on her lower lip.

The silence around her waited as if it were alive.

James squirmed, twitching first one shoulder and then the other.

With a rush of surprise, DJ felt sorry for him. He was having a harder time apologizing than she was—and she had hated every minute of it.

"I'm sorry I started the fight with DJ." The words burst out.

"Then there'll be no more incidents like this?"

Both DJ and James shook their heads.

"Consider yourselves both on probation. Any more such displays and you'll suffer the consequences."

DJ could hardly hear the words, even though she saw Bridget's lips moving. James had admitted he provoked the fight! That took guts. More guts than she'd thought he had. She watched him nod and walk out the door.

"DJ." DJ stopped in her tracks.

"Yes, ma'am?"

"I expected better of you."

"Me too." But Bridget's words cut into DJ's heart.

"Is there something going on that you would like to tell me about?"

DJ shook her head. Why would Bridget care that Gran had gone out with Joe five times in the last week? And that DJ had had a knock-down drag-out fight with her mom? And that Amy and everyone else but her got to ride and show this summer? "I better get back to work."

"If I can help in any way, I would like to." The words followed DJ out of the office. Why was she having trouble seeing the writing on the duty board? She dashed a hand across her eyes. *Must be allergies. There's too much dust around here.*

Gran's minivan was gone when DJ rode her bike up to the house. She dug in her pocket for her key to let herself in the front door, leaving her bike leaning against the side of the house. *Remember to put it away*, she reminded herself. *You don't need to get yelled at again.*

She heard the phone ringing as she finished fiddling with the key in the lock. Why, oh why did she always have trouble with the key? On the fourth ring, she finally opened the door and dashed across the room. The message machine was already asking the caller to leave a message. DJ clicked it off with one hand and lifted the receiver with the other.

"Hi, DJ speaking." She listened for a moment. "No, I'm sorry, my mother isn't here right now. Anyway, I don't think she wants the house painted. Gran and I did it last summer." She hung the phone up and read the message left for her.

Gran would be back late; she'd gone into San Francisco on BART to meet Joe for dinner. BART was the rapid-transit train that linked Bay area cities by rail.

DJ crinkled up the paper and tossed it in the trash. *Great!* Now on top of everything else, she'd have to cook dinner—unless, of course, her mother wanted to eat out. She checked the calendar. No, Mom would be at class tonight. And most likely, she wouldn't come home first.

She could call Amy and invite herself over there for dinner. Mrs. Yamamoto always said to come anytime. One more didn't make much difference, since there were already four kids. But if someone asked her about her summer . . . well, maybe it was better to stay home.

DJ wandered into the family room. The house wore

that empty, forgotten smell it had when both Mom and Gran were gone. DJ lifted the cloth draped over her grandmother's latest painting. She hadn't gotten very far today. DJ shook her head. Gran wasn't thinking too well lately, and it showed.

She ambled back into the kitchen and opened the refrigerator door. There weren't even any good leftovers. Usually when Gran was going to be gone, she made something that could be reheated in the oven or the microwave.

The quiet settled on her shoulders like a heavy blanket. A sigh escaped. She took out a can of soda and, after shutting the door with her foot, filled a glass. The soda fizzed, one side running over, so she had to slurp it quickly. The clock clicked. She'd never noticed it before.

She climbed the stairs to her room, one hand trailing on the banister. "This is a good time to work on my own art." Her voice echoed in the stairwell.

But even with charcoal in hand, her mind kept drifting back to the Academy. Why had she lost it like that with James? Some kind of Christian she was to want to beat up another human being! That is, if you could call James a human being.

DJ rolled over on her back. "How come the harder I try, the worse I get?" She curled back on her side. "God, I really want to be good and gentle, like my Gran. I hate it when someone is mad at me. That jerky James! He makes me so mad. I'll bet you'd get mad at him, too, if you were here." She hugged her knees and waited. It was so quiet. Even the birds were taking a break.

"I should have just walked away. Gran says to be extra nice to people who are mean to you. I really blew it this time. All I do anymore is blow it." She reached for a tissue in the drawer in her nightstand. The box was empty. She wiped the drip from her eye on the edge of her seafoam green bedspread. *If only Gran were here.*

"Darla Jean Randall!"

DJ jerked awake. Night had fallen. Her mother was home. "What?" She pushed herself to her feet and scrubbed her eyes with her fists. She could hear her mother downstairs.

"Your bike, that's what! How many times have I told you to put it away? You know someone could steal it. I should just let that happen—then what would you do?"

DJ flinched as if each word were a switch lashing at her legs. "I'm sorry." She swallowed the *I didn't mean to* and clattered down the stairs. On her way out to the garage, she paused at the dining room where her mother was going through the mail.

"How was your class?"

"Fine. Where's Gran?" Lindy tossed a couple of envelopes to the side.

"Out to dinner with Joe."

"Any messages?"

"No." DJ continued out to the garage. Talking with her mother was a real kick. If Gran had been there, she'd have asked about DJ's day. But not *her* mother. DJ put her bike away and closed the garage door. Her stomach rumbled when she stepped back into the kitchen. She got out the bread, peanut butter, and strawberry jam. Some dinner this had turned out to be.

The lights were out in the dining room. The family room was empty. She could hear her mother moving around upstairs in her bedroom. DJ took her sandwich and milk up to her own bedroom and shoved the door shut with her foot. What a totally crummy day!

Saying her prayers didn't make her feel any better.

"Mornin', darlin'." Gran greeted her as though nothing had happened. "You want scrambled eggs for breakfast?"

"No. I'm in a hurry." DJ grabbed a food bar out of the cupboard. "See you."

Gran came to the door to the garage. "Joe invited all of us to his house for dinner on Sunday to meet his family."

"I have a show." DJ swung aboard her bike and pedaled away. "Why'd I want to meet his family?" she muttered to herself while pumping up the street. "Who cares? I've got more important things to do than that."

"Have you been watching Megs' legs?" Bridget joined DJ at the mare's stall.

"Sure."

"Well, check that off foreleg. There's some swelling there. I saw her limping yesterday when I turned her out, so I iced it last night."

DJ stroked the bay mare's nose and squatted down to examine the leg. Sure enough, the pastern was swollen. "Sorry, girl. I'll get the ice packs." She rose to her feet and turned to leave the stall.

"I'm sorry, DJ. You want to ride Jake?"

DJ shook her head. "He'd probably come up lame, too." Now she couldn't even take her jumping lessons. The one thing in her life that seemed to be going right. Angry, she muttered a word her Gran would be shocked at. It only made her feel worse.

12

"I'M SORRY, DJ, WE'RE GOING TO HAVE TO postpone the party."

"That's okay. You can't help it that your boy has the chicken pox. We'll be glad to bring the pony when he's better." DJ hung up the phone. "That's the second cancellation. We had to run into an epidemic of chicken pox! How am I ever going to earn enough money for a horse at this rate?" She slammed her fist on the telephone stand, making the pencils in the holder jump and spill onto the floor.

"DJ, are you all right?" Gran called from the other room.

"I'm fine! Just fine!" DJ knelt and picked up the scattered pens and pencils. *If I get any more fine, I'll explode.* She dialed Amy's number and waited while Amy's brother went to get her.

"Bad news. Both our parties are canceled for Saturday—chicken pox."

"Have you ever had them?" Amy sounded funny.

"I guess. Why?"

"Because John is breaking out in spots and I never have, that's why."

"Oh, great. So, you sick or what?"

"No, not yet. But Mom says I probably will be in ten to fourteen days. I don't want the chicken pox."

DJ flinched at the wail in Amy's voice. She glanced at the calendar. *Two weeks!* That was the weekend of the Danville Saddle Club show, one of the biggest in the area.

"Maybe you won't get them. Come on, Ames, you can pray for that. I will."

"I'd rather get them now than later. Spots all over my face—yuk!"

"Yeah, and you hardly ever even have a zit." DJ twined the phone cord around her fingers. "So, how's John taking it?"

"He's too sick to care. Mom says the older you are, the worse you get it."

Visions of John covered with pussy sores made DJ cringe. "I gotta go. Talk to you tomorrow." She hung up the phone and turned to find Gran standing in the door.

"So you don't have any parties on Saturday?"

DJ shook her head.

"I'm sorry for that, but your new schedule will work out well for Joe and me. We'll have the barbecue on Saturday instead."

DJ watched as Gran lifted the receiver. Her face turned into all-over smiles when Joe answered the phone. Why, she looked as sappy as some of the girls at school who claimed to be in love. If that was what love did to a person, DJ wanted no part of it.

Gran can't be in love. She hardly knows the guy. But there she was, calling him *darlin'*. But then Gran called everyone *darlin'*. Well, not everyone—just her family. DJ and Lindy. And now Joe.

DJ felt like heaving. What was happening to her grandmother? She tried to get Gran's attention. But waving arms and making faces didn't work. Gran just smiled that sappy smile, laid a finger over her lips, and kept right on talking to Joe. Shouldn't he be at work? Wasn't there a law against calling a policeman when he was on duty? DJ stomped from the kitchen and up to her room.

"I don't want to go to a barbecue at Joe's house! I don't want to even *see* the man ever again! I don't . . ." She paused before slamming her fist into her pillow a third time. "I don't want Amy to get the chicken pox!"

How could a summer that started out so great turn into such a disaster? Diablo to ride and show in equitation and dressage. Jumping classes. Ways to earn money for a horse of her own. The best summer ever! Now it was all a bust.

She flopped across her bed and let her arms dangle over the other side. Even sketching horses wasn't fun anymore. How could she ever ride in the Olympics, when she couldn't even get through the summer? She pounded her fist on the carpet, keeping time with her swinging feet. What a mess—bam! What a mess—bam! Four beats. Wait—she'd forgotten about James accusing her of stealing the saddle and bridle. What a mess—bam!

"That bad, darlin'?" Gran stood at the door.

DJ swallowed. And swallowed again. Her eyes burned. *Bam! Don't call me "darlin'," not when you call that—that man—the same thing.* But all she said was, "I'll live."

"Guess I didn't realize livin' was in question."

DJ refused to rise to the gentle humor. What a mess—

bam! But when she heard Gran make her way back downstairs, she wanted to run after her and bury her head in Gran's lap. To tell her how awful everything was. To let her make everything all right again.

"What's with you today?" Amy planted her fists on her hips and stood, legs spread, as if to keep DJ from running right over her.

"Nothing."

"Right. And I'm Ronald McDonald. Come on, DJ, you've been ugly as sin the last couple of days. This isn't like you, not one bit."

DJ kept on brushing Megs, using long strokes with such a heavy hand that the horse turned to look at her. Dust motes flew in the sunlight from the open doorway. Megs stamped her foot and swished her tail when DJ failed to swirl the hair at her flank.

"DJ, this is your best friend, Amy, remember me? What gives?"

DJ dropped the brush and rubber currycomb into the pail. "You really want to know? Well, tomorrow I have to go to a barbecue at *Captain* Joe Crowder's house to meet his family. Sunday I get to help all of you who own your own horse at the horse show. I don't get to show, mind you—I get to *help*." She unsnapped the crossties and turned Megs around to take her out to the hot walker. "You want more?" She stopped and looked back at her friend.

Amy stood in the same spot, hands now at her side. Even in the shadow, DJ could see two tears leave Amy's almond eyes and spill down her cheeks.

DJ bit her lip. "And now even my best friend hates me. But that's no problem, because I don't like me either." She dashed away a piece of dirt that was making her eye water. "Come on, Megs. *Someone* around here should get what she wants. And you want to be outside."

What a creep you are! DJ couldn't think of any names black enough to call herself. When she returned, Amy was nowhere in sight.

Since she and Amy didn't have any pony parties on Saturday due to the chicken pox, DJ spent the early afternoon cleaning tack for the show on Sunday.

"Cat eyes," James hissed when he rode by her on the way out to the arena to practice.

While DJ heard him, ignoring him was easy. She had too far up to reach to answer. Once, she'd heard the saying *lower than a slug's belly*. It fit her now.

Amy came, did her chores, and left without saying a word to DJ. Round and round DJ moved the rag, dipping it back in the saddle soap, then round and round some more. One thing was sure, there was always plenty of leather to clean.

"Need some help?" Hilary sat down on the bale beside DJ.

"Sure." DJ nodded to the waiting pile of tack. "I hang 'em up when I'm done."

"I know the drill." They rubbed in silence. They could hear observers commenting on those still practicing in the rings for the show. A horse snorted. Another whinnied.

"How's Megs?"

"Seems okay now." Rub, dip, and rub some more.

"You helping tomorrow?"

"Yep." DJ flexed her shoulders and sat up straight.

"I had a summer like yours once."

That caught DJ's attention. *How does she know everything that's going on?* "Sure you did."

"I broke my arm, my horse went lame, and my mom and dad separated." Hilary stopped rubbing. "I was thirteen; it was a rough time anyway."

"So?"

"So, what?"

"So what happened?"

"My arm healed, my horse recovered, and my parents got back together. We were lucky. Or as my mom says, 'God took good care of us.' "

"You believe that?" Rub, dip, and rub. DJ wanted to watch Hilary's face, but she couldn't.

"Sure do. But it hurt as if I were dying at the time."

Hilary stood to hang up a bridle. She reached down and took the one DJ had just finished. "When you thank God for what's going on—no matter how bad it seems—it gets easier."

"Thanks?" DJ's voice sounded like that of a cornered mouse.

Hilary nodded. "I know it doesn't make sense, but it works. Try it and let me know what happens." She patted DJ on the shoulder. "Gotta run. See you tomorrow."

DJ checked her watch. Today was not a good day to be getting home late. And she still had to take a shower.

Gran looked as if she'd swallowed the sun—she couldn't quit shining. "You better bring a jacket; it could be foggy in San Francisco."

DJ already had hers lying by the door. Thanks to direct orders from her mother, she wore a long-sleeved green cotton shirt and tan dress pants. It was the nicest outfit she owned. When she'd suggested clean jeans and a new T-shirt, the look she got from her mother quickly changed her mind.

Everyone else would probably be in jeans. Everyone but her mother and Gran, that is.

DJ put on her earphones and plugged them into her portable cassette player as soon as she got in the car. This way she wouldn't have to talk—or listen. Or think, for that matter. One foot bobbed in time with the music. When they parked in front of a two-story house with big bay windows like many San Francisco houses, she shut off her recorder and stared. There was no yard on either side of the house—in fact, there was no place to walk between them, the walls butted right up against each other.

"Nice place," she muttered in as sarcastic a tone as she could dig up.

Her mother pinched DJ's underarm and hissed in her ear. "Shape up!"

DJ clapped her mouth shut. How could she smile and be pleasant when Gran and Joe were kissing in front of everybody? Worse still, DJ was the oldest kid there. All the others were still in grade school or younger.

Gran took DJ's hand. Joe held the other—Gran's, that is. "Come on, darlin', we want you to meet the family."

By the time DJ had met two of Joe's three children and their kids, she felt as though she were caught in a memory game time warp.

The oldest, Robert, had a pair of five-year-old twin boys named Billy and Bobby. *What yucky names,* DJ thought.

"Our mom went to heaven," Billy announced. Or was it Bobby?

"Oh." *What do you say to that?*

"Do you like horses?" Bobby asked. Or was it Billy?

"Yes, I do."

"Good, 'cause my grandpa said you'd take me for a ride."

"Ah, sure." *Come on, DJ, loosen up. They're just kids— you like kids.*

"Grandpa said you ride at an academy." A girl with shy, dark eyes stopped next to DJ.

"I'm Shawna. That's my mom and dad." She pointed to the man burning the meat and a woman holding the platter. "I'm nine."

"Hi, Shawna. I do ride."

"And you teach kids to ride."

"Some."

"Would you teach me?"

What could she say? DJ nodded. "Someday, sure." *Joe sure has been volunteering me for all kinds of things. Who does he think he is, anyway?* DJ shot him a look, but it bounced off the circle of love shining around him and Gran.

DJ rubbed her stomach. She had a really bad feeling about all this.

Shawna sat right across the table from DJ, and the twins parked themselves on either side of her. DJ felt hemmed in by munchkins. She cut into her steak. Pink juice dribbled onto her plate. These people couldn't even cook meat right! She ate around the pink part and tried to make a real meal out of the salad and corn on the cob. When she glanced up, her mother was sitting by the twins' father.

"Okay, everybody, we have an announcement to make." Joe whistled to quiet the crowd. Gran stood next to him wearing a beaming smile. "I know it's kind of sudden, but we aren't spring chickens anymore, so I'll get right to the point. This lovely lady beside me has done me the honor of agreeing to be my wife."

Wife! DJ felt her breath leave in a whoosh.*What was Gran thinking? Now her life was ruined for sure!*

13

"DOES THAT MEAN WE'LL HAVE A NEW grandma?"

"Does it, DJ?" the other twin asked.

DJ pushed back her chair. Not bothering to catch it before it hit the ground, she fled from the scene. Into the house, out the front door, down the street. She ran as if a pack of angry wolves panted at her heels.

Vaguely, over the pounding of her feet and heart, she could hear someone calling her name. Down a hill, up another. Her chest ached. Her side ached. Could a broken heart still beat? *Gran is getting married. Gran is leaving me. Am I so terrible that everyone wants to leave me?*

She leaned against a metal lamppost, her breath coming in searing agony.

"Darla Jean Randall, get in this car immediately."

It couldn't be her mother's voice. She'd left them all behind. DJ bent forward, her strangled breathing beginning to slow. "You hear me?" A person grabbing her arm accompanied the voice.

DJ twisted around and looked into her mother's angry face. Fury radiated from Lindy's eyes, her mouth, the deep lines in her cheeks. DJ noticed these as if from a great distance. She swung around and let herself be hustled into the open door of her mother's car. She sank into the seat, snapped shut the seat belt, and locked her arms over her chest.

"What is the matter with you? You've broken your grandmother's heart. And on a day that should be so happy for her! You ruined it. What a selfish brat you've become! Darla Jean, are you listening to me?"

"Sure I am. You're yelling right in my ear." *You can't make me cry. I won't let you.* The words echoed in her head and helped her clench her teeth tighter, till they felt as though they might crack.

"I think I could beat you within an inch of your life."

"Go ahead. I don't care."

"All these years Gran has cared for you—and when she needs you, you run away like a spoiled brat. And in front of all those people! I was so embarrassed I could die."

"Sure, *you* were embarrassed. Well, I'm *so* sorry. The great Lindy Randall was embarrassed." DJ wanted to stop, but words kept coming. "All those nice people, what will they think? I don't care what they think. I never wanted to meet them anyway." *I won't cry. You can't make me.*

"When we get home, I'm going to lock you in your room until you're sorry or—" Lindy swerved away from a car that she almost cut off.

"You better watch your driving." DJ wished she'd bit the words back before they leaped into the air, but biting back words didn't seem to be her skill at the moment. *I'm a real motor mouth. All this time I've been praying about my temper, and now look at me. What good has it done?* The thought made her scrunch her eyes shut. If she started to cry now, she might never stop. But one lone tear made it past her dam. One tear that slid down her face and dripped off her chin.

DJ refused to wipe it away. If she did, the rest might follow. *Gran, Mom—I'm so sorry.*

"We'll finish this discussion when we get home."

DJ sneaked a peak at her mother; all she could see were white knuckled hands clenching the steering wheel. The force of the driver's door slamming shut when they finally parked in their garage shook the whole car.

DJ stayed in the car. Maybe if she gave her mother some time alone, she'd calm down. *And maybe a comet will strike us first.* DJ sank lower in her seat. How would anyone forgive her? She'd never overreacted like this before. But when Gran got married, she'd leave them. Or what if Joe decided to move in? The thought sent her rocketing from the car. *He'd* probably just throw her in jail, claim she was a juvenile delinquent or something.

She got out and slammed the door shut. Picking up her feet took an effort. Thankfully, her mother wasn't in the kitchen, or the family room. The sounds of stirring came from upstairs. DJ stopped at the foot of the stairs. They loomed up in front of her like a mountain, and the pack she carried was too heavy to bear.

She started up. *Selfish brat—guilty. Smart mouth—guilty. Terrible temper—guilty.* One for each step of the way. All of them true. How could anyone forgive her for this mess? How could she forgive herself?

Once at the top, she started for her mother's room. She could hear the shower running. A shower was her mom's answer to everything; she said she could think better there than anywhere else.

DJ slunk into her own room and collapsed on the bed.

When she awoke, she could hear voices downstairs. She crept to the head of the stairs and sat down on the first step. The voices carried easily from the family room. Her mother, Gran, and of course, Joe.

Gran was crying.

Each sob was like a nail driving deep into the girl huddled against the wall. *I made Gran cry. I broke her heart*.

"Well, I think we should drag her down here and hash this out right now." DJ could hear her mother's pacing footsteps punctuating her speech. "We've been much too soft on her, Mother. It's my fault, I should have been around more."

"No, no . . . I just never thought she'd take our news like this." Another sniff. "And we were so happy."

"We will be, my dear, we will be. I promise you." Joe's voice rumbled.

"I'm going to get her. Now." Lindy's face appeared at the bottom of the stairs before DJ could disappear. "Good, you heard us. Now get down here."

DJ felt like a little kid caught stealing. Her grandmother had been right. Eavesdroppers never heard anything good about themselves. She rose to her feet and clumped down the stairs. By the time she reached the bottom, she knew she had to tough it out. Whatever they dished out, she could take.

But the sight of Gran's tear-washed face nearly did her in. All DJ wanted to do was run and bury her face in Gran's lap to cry out all the pain and anger. To beg forgiveness.

"I think you should be grounded for life." Her mother's words brought her up short. There would be no lap for DJ, no gentle hands brushing the hair off her forehead for a forgiving kiss. Joe stood beside Gran's chair as if to keep guard. As a policeman, he sure knew how.

"Say you're sorry."

The words stuck in her throat. Sorry didn't begin to cover how she felt.

She looked from one face to the next. Joe hated her. Her mother hated her. And Gran, who never hated anyone, looked as if her heart would never mend.

"Sit." Mom pointed to a chair in the middle of the room.

"I'll stand." DJ didn't know where the words came from. She'd been going to say she was sorry. Instead, she glared down at the chair. Where was Joe's bright light? Cops were supposed to be good at interrogating prisoners. When she raised her chin again, the steel was back in her spine.

"I wouldn't let you go to the show tomorrow, but I know Bridget is depending on you. You'll go to work and come straight home. No lessons. No riding for pleasure. I will leave a list of chores for you to do. There'll be no phone, no television, and no time with Amy—except for the pony parties. You cannot put other people at a disadvantage because of your thoughtlessness."

"Anything else?" DJ forced the words from between clamped teeth.

"Lindy, dear, you're being too hard on her." Gran's soft voice made DJ nearly crack.

"No, Mother, keep out of this. We've been much too soft on her." Lindy turned back to face DJ. "We'll discuss this again in two weeks. Is there anything you'd like to say?"

Does a condemned prisoner get any last requests? DJ squared shoulders already so stiff they ached. "I'm sorry."

Her mother shook her head. "I just wish I could believe you meant that."

"Of course she meant . . ." Gran's voice trailed off at a look from her daughter.

"May I be excused?" At her mother's nod, DJ turned and marched back up the stairs.

She woke in the middle of the night, her face wet with tears. When she got up to go to the bathroom, she paused by Gran's closed bedroom door. From inside she could hear the sounds of weeping. DJ tiptoed back to her own room. Maybe if she weren't here, everything would be better.

The sun was just tinting the sky when she finally threw back the covers and got up. There was plenty to do at the Academy before they'd be ready to trailer all the horses. At least there everyone didn't hate her. Other than James and Amy, of course. Both Gran and Mom were still sleeping when DJ silently let herself out of the house.

She threw herself into the work. She groomed horses, adjusted traveling sheets, and checked off lists to make sure all the tack was included. Loading went like a perfect drill.

She ignored the questioning look Bridget gave her and made sure she was always somewhere Amy and Mr. Yamamoto weren't. When she finally slammed the door on the van Hilary was driving, she settled in for the ride.

"You okay?" Hilary asked just before putting the van in gear.

"Sure." DJ pulled a list of the day's events from her pocket. "How many classes you entered in today?"

If she kept busy enough, maybe, just maybe, she could forget the scene in the living room the night before. Maybe she could forget her grandmother crying in the night. Maybe she could forget the fact that her best friend hadn't even said hello.

But more important, maybe she could turn off the voice inside her head that kept calling her names. Names in what sounded suspiciously like her mother's voice.

The Sunday show ran even more smoothly than the one before, which only gave DJ more time to think.

"DJ, could you look at my stirrups for me?"

DJ whirled around from the rail where she leaned her chin on crossed hands. "Sure. Have you tried?"

The little girl looked up at her as if DJ had parked her brain somewhere and forgotten to pick it up. "'Course."

"Sorry, just checking." DJ turned and walked back to the line where the horses were tied. "Okay, mount up and face me." DJ scrutinized both sides of the pony. "You sure you checked to see if your stirrups are the right length?"

A shrug was her answer. DJ smiled and shook her head. "Does the right one feel good? Great, then let's move the left up a notch." DJ followed her words with quick actions.

After patting the girl's knee, DJ glanced over to where Amy had Josh tied.

"Second call for Western Pleasure, class number eleven," came the tinny echo over the loudspeaker.

Amy mounted and trotted down the fence line to join the other contestants waiting by the entry gate.

"Go get 'em, Ames. You can take this one." DJ whispered the words to empty air.

When she watched the English Pleasure class, DJ was certain she and Diablo would have taken first. The pair that won, while competent, just didn't have the flair that she and Diablo had had. Oh, how she missed him! Watching from the sidelines was eating her alive.

"DJ, would you check with the registrar and see if Sondra is listed on the next class? Oh, and make sure James is listed in trail riding. He was trying to back out of it." Bridget handed DJ a list of contestants from the Academy.

"Sure." If James and his filly could back around the rails as well as he backed out of work, they'd win for sure. The thought made her wish she could share the joke with Amy.

The end of the day brought both relief and dread. She'd made it to the end of another show she couldn't compete in—and now she had to go home. She dragged out putting things away as long as she could. All the horses were fed, watered, and hayed. *Cut it out, DJ, you're stalling.* Her frustration goading her, she hopped on her bike and headed for home.

"Well, I hope you're happy." Her mother met her at the door.

"Now what did I do?"

"Because of your infantile actions yesterday, Joe and

Gran have called off the wedding."

"But . . ."

"Darla Jean Randall, I am so ashamed of you."

"My name is DJ." *And you can't be any more ashamed of me than I am.*

14

IF I RAN AWAY, WHERE WOULD I GO?
The buzzing of the alarm jolted her wide awake.

The thought hadn't been a dream actually; it felt more like a prodding. Must be pretty serious when even her subconscious thought about it. Maybe that was the easiest solution. They'd all be better off without her to worry about. Gran could get married so she and Joe would be happy. Mom wouldn't have to worry about finding a place to live big enough for the two of them. At least she'd be out of their hair. And there was no horse for her to worry about leaving.

DJ buried her face in her pillow. Where would she go? How much money did she have?

She threw back the covers and crossed the room to her desk. Pulling her money box out of the center drawer, she set it on the desk and lifted the lid. Her bankbook read $345.88. She counted the bills and change. Another $36 and some change. A total of $382 and—she scrambled for the exact count—seventy-seven cents. How long could she possibly live on that?

I can get a job. I look older than I am. She peered at the face in the mirror. *I could pass for sixteen, maybe even seventeen*. But right now she needed to head for the Academy. At least there she had plenty to do and people to talk to. She stuck her bankbook in her jeans back pocket.

But when she pedaled past Amy's house, it felt as if a giant fist smacked her in the gut. Riding up the first hill took more breath than the fist had left her. She downshifted. What about the pony parties? Could Amy handle them by herself? One of her brothers would surely help her.

Catching her breath on the downhill, she pumped like crazy up the next rise. Pump and coast. That seemed to be the story of her life. All ups and downs with few flat stretches. *God, what am I gonna do?* She coasted off the paved road and into the academy parking lot. After work she would take all her money out of the bank. Tonight was as good a time as any to leave.

"DJ, you have a minute?" Bridget leaned on the fence observing as DJ finished her beginning riders' class.

"Sure." DJ turned back to her students. "Okay, time to walk your horses to cool them out, then head for the area behind the barn. Another class needs the arena." She swung the gate open and smiled up at her girls.

"When are we going up in Briones again?" Krissie stopped halfway through the gate.

"Ah-h-h, soon. I'll let you know next lesson." DJ forced her mouth into a smile. She wouldn't be here to take them up in the park again. Once she closed the gate, she joined Bridget at the rail.

"You really are good with them. One of the mothers told me her daughter keeps her room clean now just because you told her neatness is a key to performing well."

Bridget turned so she was leaning against the aluminum rail.

"Thanks. I like teaching." DJ copied Bridget's pose.

"You want to tell me what has been bothering you?"

DJ blinked. She thought she'd been keeping her thoughts to herself, not skywriting them for all to see. "Ah—just home stuff. It'll all work out." She could feel the heat flaming up her neck. One thing Gran had drummed in her head—never lie or cheat.

"Remember, I am here for you when you need me." Bridget hooked a heel over the bottom rail. And waited.

DJ fought the tide of tears that threatened to swamp her. She swallowed, then swallowed again, her hands clenched by her side. *How can I just disappear when she counts on me? How can I stay? This is a mess!* The thoughts burst over each other in a confusing rush. *I can't stay—I messed up Gran's life. I'm so selfish.* She blinked herself back to the arena. "I'm sorry, I didn't hear you."

"I asked if you checked out the new gelding I put in Diablo's stall? I have assigned him to you for exercise. His name is Dandy Son, but he answers to Patches. His family only plans on being out here on the weekends. He needs training so their ten-year-old can ride him. Think you can take care of that?"

"I'll do my best."

"I have every confidence in you, DJ." Bridget started to walk away. "Let me know when you are ready to bring him out. We will see what he knows and set up a program for him." She nodded at a call for the telephone. "I will be right there. Oh, and, DJ, he is trained for Western riding."

DJ checked on her students and sent them all to dismount and groom their horses. None had worked up a sweat, thanks to the cool breeze.

She worked her way down the line of nodding horses until she came to Diablo's old stall. These stalls were supposed to be James' responsibility, but none had been forked out. And as usual, James was not in sight.

DJ shook her head. A dark brown horse, nearly black, but with a splotch of white between his eyes, came forward to sniff her hand. DJ rolled back the barred upper half of the stall door and took hold of his halter. "So, you're Patches, are you?" The gelding snuffled up her shoulder to her hair. DJ stood quietly and let him explore her. "You are a beauty, you know that?" Her soft voice and soothing hands worked their magic, aided by the carrot she dug out of her pocket.

While he crunched, she slid back the lower door and entered the stall. He stood a bit over fifteen hands, with one white sock in front and another on the opposite back leg.

When she bent down to check his legs, he rumpled her hair. "You're a bit of Arab, but what's the rest? Morgan? Quarter Horse?" He pricked his ears and nudged her shoulder. "Yeah, I like you, too. Somebody bought themselves a fine animal, didn't they?" *If only I could be here to train you.*

She felt that even more painfully after the riding session. Patches had a nice gait, easy to sit to, but with only two speeds—walk and run. He seemed willing, but he didn't know much more than simple neck reining. He also tended to get hyper when she asked him to do something unfamiliar, such as backing up or going at a gentle lope.

After she put him away, she decided to write Bridget

a letter and leave it in the office.

Amy worked on the other side of the barn, cleaning her stalls and grooming horses. But she never came out to watch the new mount or swap jokes the way she usually did.

When DJ dared to sneak looks at her used-to-be friend, she could tell Amy wasn't any happier than she was. Guess she'd have to write a note to Amy, too.

By the time DJ'd gotten her money out of the bank, it was late. She pedaled like crazy for home, not looking forward to explaining why she was late. The list of chores covered both sides of a sheet of paper.

Gran's minivan was gone again. *Probably off seeing that stupid policeman.* DJ left her bike on the front sidewalk. She'd be gone before anyone could yell at her to put it away.

First she'd write the letters, then pack. She sat down at her desk. Should she write to Gran and Mom? She shook her head. They wouldn't care anyway. Just Amy and Bridget. She wrote fast and stuffed the sheets in the envelopes. Gran could come home anytime.

DJ packed another pair of jeans, two T-shirts, and a pair of shorts in her backpack. By the time she'd added underwear, a sweatshirt and jacket, and her toothbrush and paste, she hardly had room for food. She rummaged in the cupboard downstairs. A box of food bars, a couple apples, matches. She'd camp up in Briones for a couple nights before heading . . . DJ didn't know where. She clamped her hands on the counter. Would she ever see her family again?

She wandered into the family room and lifted the cloth on Gran's latest painting. As Gran would say, it needed work. She let the cloth drop and went to sit in

Gran's chair, letting her gaze wander around the room, saying goodbye to everything. When she finally pushed herself to her feet, she might as well have been pushing up the world.

With her sleeping bag tied on the back of her bike, a canteen slung on her shoulder and her pack on her back, she pedaled out the drive and around the corner. That way no one she knew would see her on the main street, the way they usually came.

Once at the Academy, she parked her bike behind the long barn and dropped her pack beside it. The sun had already set, and long shadows stretched across the dusty parking area. She could hear a class going on in the covered arena and another at the open arena set up for jumping. Most of the adults came in the evening after work. A horse whinnied in one of the outside stalls. Inside the barn, only an occasional snort or the rasp of hay being pulled from a rack broke the silence.

Horses came to the gates and nickered or wuffled when DJ made her way down the line. She knew them all, many of them for the four years she'd worked there. An ear scratch here, a chin rub there—Megs insisted on having her ears rubbed when DJ slipped inside her stall. DJ scratched, then wrapped her arms around the deep red neck, burying her face in the black mane.

You will not cry. "You be a good girl now, you hear?" She tickled the mare's whiskery upper lip. "Thanks for all the good jumps we made." Megs nickered when DJ left the stall.

DJ leaned against the wall. She'd say goodbye to Patches, then get out of there. After she left the letter on Bridget's desk.

Even with her heart pounding in her ears, she detected an unfamiliar sound. She stopped in her tracks, the better to hear. Was there an animal trapped in a stall? A horse down? She made her way down the aisle, past Patches, and stopped again. Nothing. Concentrating, she tiptoed so as not to make a sound, checking each box stall, always moving like a ghost. She stopped and listened again. It was coming from across the aisle. She peered into Gray Bar's stall. The Arabian filly studied her with large, calm eyes. But something light colored was huddled back in the corner.

DJ slid open the stall and slipped inside. With one hand on the filly's halter, she drew closer to the far corner.

"So what are *you* staring at, cat?"

"James!" DJ nearly jumped in surprise. "What are you doing here?"

15

"NOTHING. I CAN COME VISIT MY HORSE, CAN'T I?"

"Well, sure, but . . ."

"But nothing, just get out of here and leave me alone." His voice broke on the last syllable.

DJ stroked the filly's neck and smoothed her mane. *What was going on? James never spent time alone with his horse. He rode, practiced, did his chores, and left.* It had never occurred to her that he even liked the animal, in spite of what a beauty she was. The green-eyed monster of jealousy had attacked DJ more than once because of this superb horse.

"You did pretty good yesterday."

"Yeah, right. Best I got was a red. My dad . . ." He waved her away with a clenched fist. "Go on, will ya?"

DJ kept her attention on the horse. She was sure she'd seen tears on James' cheeks. She could hear them in his voice. She knew how rotten she felt when someone came upon her when she was crying. Crying should be a private affair. But she couldn't leave. James needed someone, that was for sure. And it looked to be her.

"But you placed in the trail-riding class, and the

show before, Gray Bar wouldn't even finish the course. All your practice and work with her showed. Your dad should be real proud of you."

DJ thought she heard him mumble, "Too drunk to care," but she wasn't sure. She didn't dare ask him to repeat himself. How could she get him to talk?

God, please help me help James. She went on stroking the filly. "What about your mom? Isn't she proud of you?"

"Why? She's never home."

"Sounds like my mom. She travels for her job and then goes to school nights for her master's degree. She's been in school ever since I can remember."

"My mother says she hates coming home."

DJ felt like James had socked her. "No, she doesn't. She can't. Not really." She wished she could grab the words back and swallow them quick.

"You think I'm stupid or something? I understand English. Especially when she's screaming at the top of her lungs."

"In front of you?" DJ could hear her voice squeak.

"Nah, I listen from the top of the stairs. My dad was drunk again . . ."

Again. This time DJ caught the words before they slipped out.

"And Mom said it was the last time. She was leaving, she'd see him in court."

DJ sank down on the shavings beside him. *What do you say to something like this?* But she didn't have to say anything. It was as though someone had pulled the plug; the words bubbled out nonstop.

"My dad threw his glass into the fireplace then—I heard it smash. He'd been drinking ever since he came home. I tried to get him to stop, but after he hit me, I stayed upstairs." James clenched his hands over his knees. "It's safer that way. If I hide, he sometimes forgets what he was yelling about—at least when he's yelling at me. But Mom said she couldn't take it anymore. I think he hit her once, but she lied and said she bumped into a door."

When he fell silent, DJ cleared her throat. "So what are you going to do?"

"Me? They're gonna send me back east to military school. Dad says I need some discipline to shape me up. Ha! He's the one who needs discipline." He turned to look at DJ. "Why does he do it—drink, I mean? He says he's sorry, but then he just drinks again."

"I don't know." A picture of Gran flitted through her mind. Even if Gran got married, she'd find time for her only granddaughter. Of course she would.

James sniffed again. "I don't want to go to military school. I don't want to leave Gray Bar. I like it here at the Academy." His voice broke. The silence lengthened. "They're going to get a divorce. They say it'll be better for all of us that way." He picked up a handful of shavings and let them tumble through his fingers.

DJ wanted to take him in her arms and hold him as Gran so often held her.

He sniffed and rubbed the back of his hand across his nose.

DJ watched him from the corner of her eye. What could she say? What could she do? No wonder he'd been such a mean kid all summer.

"I'll take care of your horse for you. When you come home next summer, she'll be better trained than ever."

"Dad says he's gonna sell her."

"Oh no!" DJ looked up at the filly, who'd lowered her head to sniff and wuffle in James' hair. "She's so beautiful. You'll never find one like her again."

"I know. But . . ." He slammed his fist into the shavings. Gray Bar threw her head up and backed away. "I hate him! I could kill my dad. And Mom's no help. All she can think about is never coming home again. I hate her, too."

DJ felt her breath leave. It left her hollow, as if she might cave in. "James, you don't mean that . . . about killing, I mean."

"No. But I hate him, I really do."

She could hear the tears running into his words. And she didn't even have a tissue. *I thought I hated Joe, but I don't. Nothing like James and his dad. God, please, I want to go home. I'm sorry I've been so hard to live with.* She crossed her arms on her knees and rested her forehead on them.

The filly made manure in the corner, filling the air with the pungent aroma. Then she came back to nuzzle James.

With one hand James reached up to rub her nose. She dropped her head lower, resting her cheek against James' shoulder.

"She can tell you're sad. Horses know more about us than we give them credit for."

"I know. And I haven't taken good care of her. That's why Dad says he's selling her. He says I don't care. That I never care about anything."

"Little does he know." Right now DJ felt like going over to their fancy house and telling that mean old drunk off.

"Thanks, DJ." James turned so he could look right at

her. "I'm sorry I called you names. And about that saddle and bridle . . . I . . . I hid it." He swallowed the words.

"You did what?" DJ jerked upright.

"I hid them. Everyone likes you, and you're so good with the other kids and the horses. I just wanted you to get in trouble for once. Like me."

"James Edward Corrigan, that was a double dumb thing to do! Why'd you . . ."

"I said I was sorry. I'll put 'em back tomorrow and tell Bridget what I did."

"I'm glad you told me."

"You gonna tell my dad?"

"No way. There is some stuff I'd like to tell him, though. And none of it's very nice." Now she was the one tossing handfuls of shavings.

"How are you going to get home?" DJ leaned back against the wall.

"Call George. He's the gardener, driver—whatever we need. I thought about sleeping here tonight." He rubbed the filly's forehead. "Would you share your stall with me, girl?" She nibbled at his hair and blew gently in his face.

"She'd probably step on you."

"No, she wouldn't. Sure wish I'd worked her harder. My dad's right, you know. I *am* lazy. I'd rather play games on my computer than most anything. But I do like riding—and showing." He pushed himself to his feet and, grabbing a handful of mane, swung up on the filly. "If they don't sell her, would you show her this fall? I know you want a horse of your own, but Gray Bar here loves to jump. She's good. Bridget says she has plenty of ability."

DJ knew her mouth made an O. She could feel her

chin smack on her chest. She closed it and shook her head. "James, I . . ."

"Just say yes." James scooted back and leaned forward to rest his chin on the filly's withers. "You could go far with her."

"If you have to sell, I wish I could buy her." She thought about the money in her pocket. It wouldn't even be a down payment on a registered Arabian like this one.

"You can use her. That way it won't cost you anything."

"Thanks. You all right now?"

"Yeah, I'm fine. Just cool."

"Guess I better get home. I'm not supposed to be out past dark."

"Me neither." James slid to the ground. "I'll see you tomorrow. They can't ship me off that fast." He gave the filly another pat and pushed back the lower door. "Uh, you won't tell the other kids about this, will you?"

DJ shook her head. "Nope. You sure you're okay?"

"Hey, I'll live. Military school can't be all bad."

"I'll write to you, tell you about Gray Bar."

"Promise?"

"Promise." DJ ducked back around the barn and hefted her backpack. She couldn't get her arms in the straps fast enough. Maybe she'd get home before they even realized she was gone.

She climbed onto her bike, hitting the pedals so hard, gravel spurted out from under her rear tire. Would she ever be able to say *sorry* enough?

16

"AND JUST WHERE HAVE YOU BEEN, YOUNG lady?"

"Mom! I thought you were on another trip." DJ knew those were the wrong words as soon as they left her mouth.

"So that made it okay for you to be out after dark? Wasn't there something about being grounded?" Her mother stood in the door, fists on hips, ready to do battle. "Why do you have your sleeping bag? And a backpack? Darla Jean Randall, what in the world is going on?"

Gran ducked past her daughter's arm. "Oh, darlin', what kind of mess have you gotten into now?"

Joe filled what was left of the open doorway.

DJ wished the earth would just open up and swallow her whole. "Why'd you call in the police?"

"He's not the police . . ."

"I'm here only because I care, DJ. No other reason." Joe laid a hand on Gran's shoulder, much as DJ would gentle a horse.

"Where were you going?" Lindy bit out the words as if each one were too hot to contain.

DJ untied her sleeping bag and held it in front of her. "I was going to camp in Briones." She watched the blood drain from her mother's face.

"But there are rattlesnakes up there and . . . and tarantulas."

"Not to mention ticks. Am I right in assuming you were running away?" Joe joined in the accusations.

DJ nodded.

"Oh, Darla Jean, how could you?" Lindy sagged back against Joe's broad chest.

DJ squared her shoulders. Might as well get it all over with. "I figured you'd all be better off without me. I was acting like a spoiled brat. I'm sorry." She raised tear-filled eyes to Gran's. "I love you, Gran, and I don't want you to be unhappy."

Gran spread her arms wide, and DJ dropped her bag to fly into them like a baby bird back to the nest. "How could you ever think we would be better off without you? You've been my life. Caring for you gave me a reason to keep on living after Grandpa died. Darlin', you are my pride and joy."

"But . . . but now you have Joe."

"I wish," the deep voice grumbled.

"There's plenty of love to go around. Why, we'll be living right up the road from the Academy, so you can come to our house after school and when your mother is traveling. We plan to have plenty of room for grandkids."

"Huh?" DJ pulled back to look Gran in the face.

"I made an offer on a place near the Academy yesterday. Looks as though they'll take it." Joe drew the women into the house.

"My bike."

"You can let it lie there for now." Lindy's voice had lost its edge. Now she just sounded tired. "Let's sit down and hash this out." She reached for her daughter and DJ went into her arms willingly. "You scared me half to death. I should ground you for life." She sniffed and continued. "Amy didn't know where you were. Says you haven't talked to her for days. Bridget said you left earlier this afternoon."

DJ groaned. "Did you call everybody?"

"Just about. Hilary said she knew you'd been bothered about something lately."

"I'm sorry, Mom. Please forgive me."

"Oh, I forgive you, all right, but there are some serious consequences here. You could have gotten lost or murdered or kidnapped or . . ."

"I get the picture. Will a promise to never do something so stupid again help?"

Gran and Joe sat down on the couch, holding hands like two kids. Lindy took Gran's wing chair, and DJ folded herself down to the floor.

"Now, then. Start from the beginning and tell us what's been on your mind."

"Easy, Joe. She isn't a delinquent, you know." Gran squeezed his hand and laid her head against his shoulder.

DJ wrapped her hands around her bent legs and did as he asked. By the time she finished, her throat felt as raw as if she'd been running during the hottest time of the day.

"Now it's your turn, Lindy. Let's get this out on the table."

By the time they'd all talked, the grandfather clock bonged eleven times.

DJ's stomach growled in time with it.

"Oh, you poor child! Didn't you have any dinner?" Gran started to rise, but Joe stopped her.

"The three of you keep talking. I'll bring something in for all of us."

When he left the room, DJ whispered, "Is he always this nice?"

"Of course, DJ, when you give him a chance." Lindy leaned forward. "Just like you didn't give any of us a chance to work things out. You panicked. Now you and I'll be living here together, just the two of us. I think learning to communicate will be rather important, don't you?" She held up a cautioning hand. "I know, I'm as much at fault as you—more so since I'm the adult. But we *will* make it."

DJ knew she should say something in response, but words seemed to have vacated her brain. She just nodded.

"I'm glad to see the two of you coming to this agreement. That's the first step. Now we need to leave the rest of it in God's hands." Gran reached out and patted their hands.

DJ scooted over by Gran. "So, when's the wedding?"

"We haven't discussed it again . . ."

"As soon as we can arrange it. Two weeks max." Joe set a plate with ham sandwiches on the table and popped open a bag of tortilla chips.

DJ squirmed at the way he butted into the conversation. But she kept her mouth closed—this time. *You're learning*, she congratulated herself. "Will I have to wear a dress?"

"As one of my bridesmaids, you sure enough will."

"What?"

"Your mother will be the other."

"And my son Robert will be the best man. Bobby and Billy thought they should be included, but we vetoed that idea."

"Sounds as if it's all planned." DJ swallowed quick so she wouldn't get accused of talking with her mouth full. Ham and cheese had never tasted so good. "Oh no!" She leaped to her feet and headed for the garage. "My bike."

"Serves you right if it's stolen," Lindy grumbled.

When DJ returned, she sat at her mother's knee. "What are you going to add to the list in there to punish me for tonight?" She figured knowing was better than guessing.

"I'm not sure yet. Once I get over wanting to strangle you, I'll think better." She leaned forward and wrapped her arms around her daughter. "I sure hope you've learned a lesson. If you do it again—"

"I won't."

"If you do, I'm going to call the police—and I know just where to start." She hugged DJ hard.

DJ snuggled closer. "What can we do about James?"

"Nothing, I'm afraid. Just be his friend. He needs one right now, that's for sure. I'm surprised he hasn't been in more trouble already."

"Military school, ugh." DJ shivered. When a yawn caught her, she covered her mouth with one hand. Even so, it traveled around the room.

"I'll be getting on home. Sure glad we're not putting out an APB on you, kid. Melanie, you want to walk me to the door?"

DJ picked up the remains of the meal and carried them into the kitchen. She glanced out the window to see Joe and Gran kissing by his car.

"Cute, aren't they?" Lindy asked from right behind her.

"Guess so." Tonight cute didn't sound quite so bad. As Gran always said, "If ya can't lick 'em, join 'em." Tonight she'd done just that.

Saying her prayers came easy. "Thank you for my room and my bed. Sure beats the rocks in Briones. And for Mom and Gran—and Joe, too. But, God, I'm kind of scared. There are just so many changes happening." She paused to think. "And help James. Amen." She didn't include her nightly request for a horse this time. Not asking was part of her punishment. And in the morning she had to make up with Amy, if Amy was willing.

"God, please help me talk to Amy. Forgive me for the mess I made. I really want to listen to you. Could you maybe speak a little louder, please?"

She overslept and arrived at the Academy late. James was shoveling out stalls.

"Amy is out in the arena." He leaned on the handle of his shovel.

"How ya doing?" DJ crossed to the other aisle.

"I'll live." He went back to his job. "You can ride Gray Bar later if you want."

"Thanks, but I can't. I'm grounded from pleasure riding."

"What?"

"It's a long story. But thanks for the offer. Later, all right?" At his nod, she turned and trotted out of the barn into the sunlight. She blinked and dodged just in time. Amy's horse stopped before stepping on her.

"Hey, you don't have to run me down." She shaded her eyes with her hand. "Amy, I need to talk to you."

"So talk." Amy crossed her arms over the pommel of her saddle.

"I'm sorry I've been such a dumbbell."

"Me too."

"I've missed you."

"Me too."

"Is that all you can say?" DJ ran a hand down the horse's gray neck. It was easier to study the swirls on the hide than to look up at her friend. "You still want to be my friend?"

"Of course. I just figured you wanted out. I never stopped being your friend." Amy tightened the reins to keep her horse still. "What happened?"

"Can we talk later? I'm way behind. You have no idea how stupid I've been."

"You said it, not me." She nudged her horse forward and into the shadow of the barn. "Bridget wants to see you," she called over her shoulder.

"Okay." DJ started toward the office but turned and trotted down the aisle to see Patches first. At least she'd have him to train and she could jump James' Arab. That ought to give her time to earn some more money for her own horse.

"Hi, fella, you miss me?" She rubbed the gelding's swirled white patch. Digging a carrot out of her pocket, she fed him and told him how handsome he was. "Gotta go. I'll be back to clean your stall in a bit."

"DJ, your mother called me." Bridget pointed to the chair beside the desk. "She said you are grounded from riding for a month but can do your regular chores around here. Is that correct?"

DJ stared at a spot above Bridget's head. "Yeah, but

I can still train horses. I'm only grounded from riding for pleasure and classes."

"I see. Well, you know how I feel about self-discipline." She waited for a nod from DJ. "I believe we learn best by accepting our mistakes. So, to help you remember yours so you won't do them again, I have assigned Patches to Hilary for training. Megs will be turned out to pasture for a month. That should give her leg time to heal. Is there anything you would like to say?"

DJ clamped her jaw and shook her head. She *couldn't* say anything.

17

*BY THE TIME I CAN RIDE AGAIN, SCHOOL WILL
start. I won't get to show in the Labor Day Horse show.*
"What a zero for a summer."

"Tough break?" Hilary fell in step beside her.

"You don't know the half of it." DJ sucked in a deep
breath. The rock in her throat made it difficult.

"You'll get through it. I can feel in my bones that
something good is coming for you." Hilary turned and
walked backward. "And my bones never lie."

Her effort at making DJ smile nearly worked.

By the time she finished her usual work and the extra
stalls Bridget had assigned her, DJ longed for a cold
soda. But she'd left all her money at home in her box
until she could put it back in the bank. The hose would
have to do. She ran it until it was cold, drank, and
washed off her arms. If only she could go riding, she'd
feel better. Right now she understood what jail might
feel like.

At least it was old times for her and Amy. They rode
their bikes home, promising to talk later.

"Oh, I forgot. I can't!" DJ wailed. "You're on my

grounded list. Unless we have a pony party, which we do tomorrow."

"Great." Amy shook her head. "When you mess up, you really mess up."

The next morning James wore a face that dug a furrow in the dirt. "They're not selling my horse."

"That's great!" DJ slapped him on the shoulder.

"They're shipping her back with me to the military school so I can join the equestrian program. I'm sorry, DJ, I was hoping you could train and jump her."

DJ swallowed the disappointment. Maybe God didn't think she needed a horse after all. "That's okay, thanks for the thought." She kicked a piece of crushed rock off to the side. "You know when you leave?"

"School starts the day after Labor Day, so I'll miss the show. You said you'd write."

"I will. I better get to work. Don't worry, James. Hilary said something good is coming my way." *And I just wish it would get here.*

The time before the wedding flew by in spite of the strict rules DJ's mother had laid out for her. Gran painted, cooked, and sewed in a daze. One afternoon she took DJ shopping.

"You need school clothes and a dress. I think a long dress would look lovely on you."

"A dress?" DJ slumped in the car seat. "I hate dresses, you know that."

"For *my* wedding, you will wear a dress. And since Joe is in such a rush that I don't have time to sew one, we'll do the shop 'til we drop routine."

I'm dropping already. But DJ was learning to keep her mouth shut. After all the trouble she caused Gran, at least she could wear a dress. She didn't have to like it, though. "No ruffles and lace."

"All right. No ruffles and lace." Gran patted DJ's knee. "But that'll probably make for a longer shopping trip."

DJ groaned.

They started at the Sun Valley Mall and ended up at the Broadway Plaza in Walnut Creek.

"My feet hurt." DJ collapsed on a chair in a coffee shop.

"At least your feet are young. What about mine?" Gran propped her elbows on the table. "We're about out of stores, darlin'. If we don't find something at Nordstrom's, we'll have to go down to Stoneridge Mall or into the city."

DJ laid her head down on her crossed arms. "We bought enough school clothes. You know I hate shopping, and I hate shopping for a dress even more." She raised her head enough for a half-hearted grin. "But if I have to shop, going with you is the best. Thanks for my new school clothes."

But even she bit her tongue when she looked in the mirror a while later. It *was* the perfect dress. The deep aqua made her eyes sparkle and the simple lines disguised her flat chest. She looked grown up.

"Wow."

"Darla Jean, I knew you would be a beauty someday. I think someday is now." Gran smoothed a hand over the gauzy fabric.

DJ could see Gran was fighting back tears. "Come on, Gran. It's just me, horse-crazy DJ." But even she couldn't help taking an extra twirl just to feel the cloth swish about her legs. "Bummer."

"Now what?"

"Now I need new shoes."

Gran laughed in her tinkly I'm-really-happy voice. "Shoe department, here we come!"

By the day before the wedding, DJ and Amy had given three more pony parties, worked extra hours at the Academy, and tried to keep Gran on track. For the first time in her years of illustrating, she was behind on a deadline.

"Just call 'em and tell 'em you're getting married. You'll finish the book later." DJ sucked in half a can of soda in a single chug.

"I can't do that." Gran peered at the half-finished painting. "I'm just not happy with this one."

"Don't worry, Gran. Being in love makes everyone looney."

"How would you know?" She daubed some darker green on one of the trees.

"Television, movies. Sappy looks go with the territory." DJ hurriedly left the room when her grandmother threatened her with a paintbrush. She returned a bit later with a flat package all wrapped in silvery wedding paper. "Here, I can't wait 'til tomorrow."

Gran sat in her chair and carefully removed the ribbon. "Just rip it." DJ sat in front of her, legs crossed.

Smiling, Gran shook her head. "It's not every day one

gets to open wedding gifts. I'm going to enjoy every minute." At last the paper fell away and she held the framed picture in her hands.

"I didn't know what to get you."

"This couldn't be more perfect." The jumping horse and rider was DJ's best picture ever. She'd colored it with pastels. Even all the shading had come out right.

"I'll hang this in a place of honor." Gran held the frame up to catch the morning light. "You chose a perfect mat and frame to set it off. Darlin', you have a real flair for this."

"They helped me over at Frame City." The seventy-five dollars it had cost had sure hurt her bank account. But she'd wanted it to be perfect.

Gran set the picture aside and placed both hands on DJ's cheeks. "Nothing you could give me could mean more. I know Joe will agree with me. Thank you." She brushed away the tears that threatened to spill over. "My, I sure have turned into a waterworks lately. I better get back to my own pictures."

But Gran had her paintings finished, boxed, and ready to ship by the next morning. Her suitcases were mostly packed when DJ came yawning down the stairs.

"Did you sleep at all, Mother?" Lindy folded one more garment into the waiting luggage before zipping them all shut.

"Thank you, my dear." Gran yawned. "I never would have made it without your help."

"This is just terrific—the bride is so tired she's collapsing before the wedding." Lindy looked around the room in case she was forgetting something. "Darla Jean, you need to get a move on. I'll do your hair if you like."

"My hair? I thought I'd wear it in a snood, like I do

for the shows." DJ backed away.

"Some curls would be nice, you know. We could pull it back on the sides and leave it in curls down the back." Lindy's hands described the style. "We bought you flowers to wear, too."

DJ groaned. "I think I'm going to be sick."

"Speaking of sick, Mrs. Yamamoto called. Amy broke out this morning, so she won't be at the wedding. And no, you can't go over there. We don't have time."

DJ felt her face. What if she broke out in the chicken pox today, too? Then she could stay home. She shook her head. No, she didn't want to miss the circus.

But it wasn't a circus. She led the way down the aisle at their brick-walled church. Straight ahead, over the altar, Jesus cuddled a group of children in a stained-glass window that glowed in the sunlight. Lindy followed with Gran on her arm.

DJ looked up to Joe in time to see two tears glisten on his cheeks. Gran took his arm and smiled up at him. As they stood in the golden light from the window, it shone like a special blessing.

"Dearly beloved," the minister began. "We are gathered here in the sight of God and this company . . ."

DJ fought a lump in her throat. This wouldn't be happening if God didn't want it to. Gran had prayed for all of them. DJ added her own request. *God, please make Gran happier than she's ever been. I love her so much.* Crying at weddings was silly—wasn't it?

Gran said her vows in her soft southern accent, all the love of creation shining in her eyes.

DJ heard her mother sniff. She didn't dare look at her. *I am not going to cry.*

"You may kiss the bride." The minister's words

brought an end to the ceremony. "I am proud to introduce to you Mr. and Mrs. Joe Crowder." Gran and Joe turned to face the congregation and everyone clapped.

They really did look nice together, Joe so tall and silvery, Gran so small and golden. DJ sniffed in sync with her mother. The music burst forth in applause as Gran and Joe started back down the aisle, shaking hands with friends and relatives as they went. Lindy took the arm of Robert, Joe's oldest son, and smiled up at him through her tears. DJ took the younger son's arm.

"You look like a million dollars, DJ," Andy whispered as they left the sanctuary.

"Thanks to Gran." DJ stood straighter and smiled up at him. Did this make him her uncle? They followed the newlyweds down the aisle and out the door.

The reception was being held in the fellowship room, one building over.

"DJ, we was quiet, wasn't we?" The twins each grabbed a handful of her dress. "Daddy said if we be good, you could take us for a ride on Bandit someday."

DJ stooped over and gave each of them a hug. "I surely will." Funny how she needed to hug someone, as if there was so much love sloshing around inside her it might run out. Is this what weddings did for people?

"Today?" Bobby—or was it Billy—asked hopefully.

"Sorry, not today, but soon." She looked from one beaming face to the other. "How am I gonna tell you two apart? I know, you . . ." She pointed to the one on her right.

"Bobby." He supplied her with a name.

"You have a freckle on the end of your nose."

"Are you sure it's not frosting?" Their father appeared at her side. "The newlyweds are looking for you."

He pointed across the room. "Over there."

"Thanks." DJ made her way through the crowd to where Gran and Joe were accepting best wishes, along with bunches of hugs and laughter. Just standing by them made DJ feel bubbly.

"Oh, there you are, darlin'." Gran drew DJ into one of her special hugs and whispered in her ear. "Thank you for looking so lovely and for being my maid of honor. I'm so proud of you."

DJ couldn't disguise a sniff this time. "I miss you already."

"But I'll be back soon. Joe has something to ask you. He was going to wait 'til later, but he's as bad as I am when it comes to keeping secrets." She wiped her eyes with a tissue and tucked another into DJ's hand.

DJ turned to the man standing behind her. She reached out to shake his hand, but instead, put her arms up for a hug. She could hear both her mother and grandmother sniffing now. At the rate they were going, they'd all be in tears soon. Including her.

"Thank you, my dear. You've made your grandmother very happy today." He kept an arm around her shoulders and eased her over closer to the wall. "I have kind of a suggestion, or a . . . a . . ."

DJ looked at him with a question. Surely a police captain wasn't having a hard time saying something? "A. . . ?" She tried to help him.

"Well, you heard me talk about Major?"

DJ nodded. "Your horse on the mounted patrol."

"He's going to retire with me, but he has a lot of good years ahead of him, good working years. I just thought maybe he'd be a good horse for you—if you're willing, that is."

"W-willing? Major would be mine?"

Joe nodded. "Melanie says you'd have to pay for him. Something about learning responsibility."

"I only have four hundred dollars."

"That's right about what I thought would be good."

"Major would be mine."

"As soon as I retire, in another month."

"I will have a horse of my own." If she said the words often enough, maybe she would begin to believe them. Hilary had been right. Something good *was* coming her way. She not only had a grandfather and a whole new family, but a horse of her own. A horse named Major. Get ready, Olympics. DJ Randall was on her way!

DJ's Challenge

DJ Randall and her mother, Lindy, are struggling to create a happy family life now that Gran has remarried and moved away, but the situation seems hopeless. Suddenly, Lindy drops a bombshell—she's considering a position with an L.A.-based company. DJ is devastated. If they move, she may not be able to keep Major! Find out what happens in Book #2 of the HIGH HURDLES series.

Acknowledgments

My thanks to Joanie Jagoda for her expert horse-woman's critique and suggestions.

Early Teen Fiction Series From Bethany House Publishers
(Ages 11–14)

—⁂—

BETWEEN TWO FLAGS • by Lee Roddy
Join Gideon, Emily, and Nat as they face the struggles of growing up during the Civil War.

THE ALLISON CHRONICLES • by Melody Carlson
Follow along as Allison O'Brian, the daughter of a famous 1940s movie star, searches for the truth about her past and the love of a family.

HIGH HURDLES • by Lauraine Snelling
Show jumper DJ Randall strives to defy the odds and achieve her dream of winning Olympic Gold.

SUMMERHILL SECRETS • by Beverly Lewis
Fun-loving Merry Hanson encounters mystery and excitement in Pennsylvania's Amish country.

THE TIME NAVIGATORS • by Gilbert Morris
Travel back in time with Danny and Dixie as they explore unforgettable moments in history.